A figure moved ⟨...⟩ ⟨th⟩at rimmed the pool and, believing it was the guard come to warn me to get out of the water, I asked, "Did a fuse blow?"

There was no answer. Something swept in an arc across the glitter of the apartment houses and connected with the side of my head. I swallowed a mouthful of water before another blow struck my shoulder. I thrust myself away from the edge, gasping for breath.

The dim figure moved again and with a kick I plunged into the deepest part of the pool.

★

TIME LAPSE

JANICE LAW

W✸RLDWIDE®

TORONTO • NEW YORK • LONDON
AMSTERDAM • PARIS • SYDNEY • HAMBURG
STOCKHOLM • ATHENS • TOKYO • MILAN
MADRID • WARSAW • BUDAPEST • AUCKLAND

To Jerry and Jamie

TIME LAPSE

A Worldwide Mystery/March 1998

This edition published by arrangement with
Walker and Company.

ISBN 0-373-26267-1

Printed in U.S.A.

TIME LAPSE

ONE

IT WAS ONE OF THOSE books that become part of the urban landscape. A fat, gaudy monolith of cardboard and paper, it stood for a season in close-packed rows across bookstore windows, then reappeared, its shiny covers slightly tashed, in the discount bins before a final paperback flourish on the supermarket racks. There the screaming adjectives—Dazzling! Shattering! Gripping!—that had greeted its original appearance were combined with statistics of the vast numbers of copies sold and the promises of a "major motion picture."

I held out in spite of these blandishments. To tell you the truth, I had other things on my mind. The economic downturn had hurt even exclusive services like Executive Security, and I was spending a lot of time contemplating red ink. But one evening I noticed that my husband had succumbed to the combined lures of Publishers' Row and Madison Avenue. Harry was sitting bowed under the weight of the eight hundred pages of spies, chases, and esoteric science contained in that immense best-seller, *The Lazarus Gambit.*

"I thought that was what used to be called 'light reading,'" I said.

Harry looked up. "What?"

"Joke, Harry. Light reading."

"My dear, million-dollar best-sellers are required to be heavy."

"That one appears to have been sold by the pound."

"Ounces, at least, but I love a good Denham. The man puts in absolutely everything."

I twisted my head to look at the dust jacket. "Sex, violence, and Nazis?" I guessed.

"Well, so we're promised. At the moment, we're hunting lungfish in prewar Uganda."

"I had no idea it involved anything so interesting."

"Good stuff, actually. Rossol will make a super movie out of it."

"Rossol? I didn't realize he was doing it. Not his usual line, is it?" Having turned two underrated scripts into smash hits, Leonard Rossol was the director of the moment.

"I suppose he wants to branch out. After all, Coppola did the *Godfather* pictures and Lukas the *Stars Wars* stuff. Why not a spy thriller?"

"I thought *Smiley's People* was the last word in spy stories."

"No sweep," said Harry.

I didn't argue; he's the artist.

"This would be quite different," he continued, "exotic sets, rallies, Berlin in flames, Argentina in rebellion—"

"Sounds like work for James Bond."

"Not necessarily. Remember Leni Riefenstahl?"

"But presumably our Mr. Rossol will be on the good guys' side?"

"It's traditional," Harry said, turning a page, "but I'm still in the prologue."

"With the lungfish in Africa."

"That's a clever touch, actually. The lungfish lives in a semidesert area and for months of the year, its ponds dry up."

"Inconvenient."

"No bother. The critter builds itself a cocoon of mud in the bottom of the pond and goes into a deep state of suspended animation."

"Fascinating, but what's our hero doing bothering it in Uganda?"

"We're not sure he's the hero yet. He's a German scientist studying hibernation, suspended animation, and low-temperature biology."

"First part of sweeping cinematic canvas: German scientist wading around with a fishnet. It sounds to me as if Rossol will have his work cut out."

"No," Harry said, "Uganda used to be a paradise. Hot, beautiful, full of animal life. High blue skies, endless savanna. Then"—his hand made a chopping motion—"cut to Berlin or wherever and the rise of the Nazis."

"Terrific, but I don't quite see the point."

"I see you haven't been keeping up with the reviews. The plot puts Hitler into suspended animation."

"Thanks to the poor old lungfish?"

"So it seems," my husband said, and, without another word, he sank down into his chair and back into the African savanna. I made a face, returned to my depressing balance sheet, and went off to bed alone.

A few days after Harry finished this tome, the Post reported a freak accident on location where *The Lazarus Gambit* was being filmed. Henry Brook, one of the stars of the picture, had been killed, and the production was in abeyance. Before the hubbub resulting from the death of ''one of America's most distinguished actors'' died away, I received a visit from a gentleman high up in one of our most distinguished insurance companies. He'd made an urgent call over the weekend and arrived in my office midmorning on Monday. When I went into our small lobby, he uncoiled himself from a chair and stood up, tall, thin, dignified, and definitely a bit gray about the gills. ''Ms. Peters.''

''Mr. Valon. How nice to see you again.'' We had worked together briefly once before on the matter of a stolen Stradivarius, and I'd found him cautious but shrewd. ''Would you like some coffee?''

He hesitated, shifted his briefcase nervously from one hand to the other, then nodded. ''Perhaps it might help, but no cream or sugar.''

I had forgotten that Valon was a martyr to the airplane. ''How was the trip down?'' I asked as I held the door to my office for him.

''Wretched as usual.'' He swallowed uncomfortably, then took out his handkerchief and wiped his damp forehead.

''Would a couple of crackers help?''

''I don't know. Well, yes, please. They'll either help or bring on the crisis.''

That, I gathered, was New England humor. ''We'll hope for the best.''

''Indeed, indeed.'' He sipped his coffee and nodded. ''I should have taken the train, but I'm needed right back.''

''I'm flattered you came all this way.''

"It was not something we could conveniently discuss by telephone and asking the president of Executive Security to the home office would have caused talk. Understand, we have a perfectly good crew handling this matter."

I nodded. The translation was that they couldn't be trusted to find matches after arson.

"It's a case quite out of the ordinary."

"So you'd mentioned." That's all he'd said over the telephone—plus that a lot of money was involved.

"It's the movie."

"The movie, Mr. Valon?"

"The *Lazarus Gambit.* You've heard of it, of course." He wiped his forehead again with a look of tortured desperation. Poor man, dignity is hard to maintain with airsickness.

"Yes," I said, secure in Harry's synopsis. "It should be quite a spectacle. It's going to be a picture with a lot of sweep."

"Exactly, so it should have been." He took another drink from his cup. "Perhaps a little more coffee?"

I fetched the pot. "Unfortunately," he said, "grandeur and sweep cost money."

"I've read there may be some difficulty finishing the production. Is that true?"

He took a sip and sighed. "I'd like to hope it could be finished. But they were exactly halfway through filming. The accident couldn't have happened at a worse moment, not if it had been timed precisely." He caught my look and shook his head. "I'm not suggesting that," he said. "No, no. Just emphasizing how bad the timing was from our point of view."

I wondered. Valon was not the sort for irrelevant

figures of speech, but I let it pass. "Expensive, too, no doubt."

"The picture was budgeted at well over forty million."

"That seems a lot of money for Nazis and moonshine."

"Location shooting, crowd scenes, four top performers—it adds up, but the film would almost surely have been profitable. I'm told it had everything going for it." He shrugged. "Not my department, fortunately, but their premiums were very satisfactory."

"And now, if everything is in order, your company has no choice but to pay up."

"The risks are part of the game, Ms. Peters. You won't mind if I have another cracker? They seem to help." He nibbled one of the Saltines and brushed a few crumbs from his immaculate wool suit. "What we at Independence Mutual don't like is any tampering with the odds. Which brings up my department."

He paused, and I waited. "My area of interest in this matter is smaller but not inconsequential. We insured the late Henry Brook as part of the overall package, but he carried an additional individual policy worth nearly a million dollars."

"Not exactly small change even in context."

"No, indeed. A claim has been filed, but we are not satisfied. Not satisfied at all. Of course, it's a delicate matter. The coroner's report leaves it as misadventure. Which simply means that a country M.D. doesn't always have the most sophisticated understanding or equipment. Were it a small claim, a poor family, we would certainly make some immediate settlement."

"Of course," I said. One of the tedious things about insurance people is their earnest pretense that they're not basically concerned with the cash.

"I realize that in any case where there are widows and orphans we look like the villains if there isn't immediate payment, but—"

"I didn't realize there was a widow."

"I was speaking generally. Mr. Brook was without dependents. His son, however, would be one of the beneficiaries. A man of twenty-five."

"Hardly a babe at the door of the orphanage," I admitted.

"And very well fixed in any case." Mr. Valon sighed. "Still, it's unpleasant. To prove our suspicions will cause distress."

"And these suspicions are?"

"That Henry Brook committed suicide."

"I see. Your policy doesn't—"

"No, no. Never suicide. Oh, for the company policy, everything is covered. With theatrical people, I'm told, one cannot cover too much."

"I'm sure."

"But on personal policies, no."

"Declining to put temptation in the way—"

"Preventing, as we prefer to say, Ms. Peters, connivance to defraud."

"And you believe that a noted actor, playing in what promised to be an immensely lucrative role, killed himself before collecting his salary?"

"Put that way, the situation is ridiculous."

"Put it another way for me."

Now Valon allowed himself a small, shrewd, humorless smile. "I don't wish to prejudice your mind,

Ms. Peters. Let's just say the situation is full of anomalies.''

"All right. Where do I fit in?"

"That is rather delicate. We'd like you to have a look around."

"Fair enough. What for?"

Valon brought the tips of his long, bony fingers together. "For whatever you can find. I trust your instincts. Specifically, I want to know if Brook could have killed himself. You will know how to go about that."

"It would be good if I had some sort of cover story. As you say, this is a sensitive area at the moment."

"We've thought of that," Valon said, tapping his fingers together lightly. "We have some specialists examining the film already shot—to see whether the picture can be salvaged if Brook's scenes are reshot or recut."

"And I could join this group?"

"Exactly. A visiting specialist, if you like, or someone we are training for the field. We can leave your precise designation a little vague."

"Whatever, so long as it gives me some leeway and doesn't require any special expertise. Where is the film?"

"In New York City, except for the final reels, which are still on location upstate with Leonard Rossol and his crew."

"I imagine this must have been a blow for him."

"So I understand. He's been very cooperative and he's managed to keep the crew together. But that won't last. They all have other commitments coming up."

"Then I'd better get there as soon as possible. I'll need to meet Rossol anyway."

"If you can leave tomorrow, you can see the remaining cast and crew."

I looked at my calendar, but that was just for show. I needed work, and a paying customer like Independence Mutual was a godsend. "I think I can squeeze that in."

"Good," Valon said. He wished me luck, shook my hand, and departed stoically for his plane. I called through to the adjoining office to have Harriet get me on the Metroliner the next day.

"Book you for the morning?" she asked.

"As early as possible." I was suddenly eager to get out of the office, with its unpaid bills and tardy customers. A trip to upstate New York in early April sounded good. A chance to poke through an unfinished movie sounded better. It looked, despite one or two little details I preferred to suppress, as if Mr. Valon and Independence Mutual had not only solved our cash flow problem but brought me a nice little holiday.

TWO

THE METROLINER PULLED AWAY with a lurch that belied its sleek and efficient interior and emerged into the gray D.C. morning. At twenty minutes after six, I was feeling genuinely virtuous as I opened my case for the paperback edition and the marked script of *The Lazarus Gambit*.

As Harry had already told me, the novel began with a journey into the interior of colonial Uganda. A little steam train moved through open, brushy plains thick with wildebeest, antelope, and lions, while at isolated stations British officers in tropical kit examined the documents of a German scientist seeking "biological specimens." This was Henry Brook's role, and had filming gone ahead, the late actor would have found himself snapping out orders to his bearers, netting lungfish in the shallow, muddy ponds of the region, and, if the script were faithful, wiping the sweat from "his handsome, sun-bronzed features."

He'd certainly have looked the part, for he'd been extremely attractive. Henry Brook had been a box office draw for nearly twenty years. More. Harry and I had just started seeing each other when Brook hit the top. Maybe that's why a certain romantic aura surrounded his films for me, but a Henry Brook picture was always a treat. And though he'd acquired some gray hair and a few extra pounds, he was still pure magic on the screen, one of those fortunate beings who make life seem more interesting and vivid than it can ever be. He was the first of my generation of big stars to die, and I'd been sorry.

Now I was puzzled. Despite the sun-bronzed features and promises of adventure, I couldn't imagine Brook in the role, and I decided to skip the rest of the remorselessly detailed African episodes and move on to Germany, where Dr. Kleinz returned to his laboratory at the University of Kiel.

There the doctor's work-obsessed character became clearer. Several telling vignettes had been selected for the film, including Kleinz's opportunistic reaction to the removal of a Jewish colleague and his contempt for a demonstration by the boorish Nazi brownshirts. Both responses were apolitical. The scientist was a man on the make, and nothing, not even his gentle fiancée, Hanna, was going to get in the way of his research.

I interrupted this depressing account to check the notes Valon had thoughtfully supplied. Hanna was played by the rising young stage actress Lani Dupres, who had been filming with Brook the day before his accident. Although she obviously had a sizable part in the movie, Hanna was dropped at this point where the novel began to concentrate on the laboratory. There every detail of lungfish life was rehearsed, along with the doctor's clever, and ultimately successful, attempts to persuade them to estivate in their newly drained tanks. The cocooned and torpid fish were decapitated, their brains removed, and an extract made from both the mid-and hind-brain areas. This was injected into groups of experimental rats, which immediately showed radical drops in their temperature, activity levels, and metabolic rates.

As Pennsylvania slid by beyond the glass, I pursued Kleinz's researches, which from this point moved swiftly and successfully, as befitted a man destined for more dramatic events. Thanks in part to the departures of other researchers with purer ethics or less pure blood, Kleinz soon headed a combined medical and biological team that produced purified samples of the hormone controlling the estivating behavior, as well as a complete analysis of the chemical. When the team published their first results, a synthetic form of the hormone seemed within reach, and the authors allowed themselves some modest speculations about the possible benefits of their discovery. Word of these possibilities brought them the attention of the sinister Heinrich Himmler, who had an interest in esoteric research. One cold, gray morning, there was a knock on Dr. Kleinz's office door, and a black-clad SS courier appeared. Dr. Kleinz was summoned to Bavaria to discuss a highly secret and important scientific venture; it was to film this meeting that Henry Brook had been in New York State.

I put the book down and rubbed my weary eyes. Ahead, Manhattan rose in smoggy glory, and from the seats around me, briefcase latches clicked and bags and parcels rustled. As we entered the smoky breath of the station, I put away the book, wondering again what it was in the cold and detached Dr. Kleinz that had tempted Brook to essay so uncongenial a character.

Penn Station is a depressing arrival point, a murky cavern resembling a disaster shelter. Among the weary travelers, wanderers, restless children, and eccentrics who slumped on the benches or slouched against the pillars, the Independence Mutual representative was easy to spot in his dark blazer and company tie.

"Oh, Ms. Peters," he said when I introduced myself, "I'd begun to worry. Ed Martins. Glad to have you on board." He glanced at my luggage. "Any special secret weapon for us?"

"I'm afraid not. Did you rent me a car?"

"Yes. Or rather, you can keep the one I have. I'm to go up to location today anyway to check the final dailies. I hope that's all right."

I had planned on a quiet ride up with time to think over the situation, but I said that was fine.

"You've been filled in?" He had quick, bright eyes and, in spite of his considerable size, an alert, inquisitive expression like a clever and aggressive squirrel. He was obviously dying to know why I'd come, as well as a trifle uneasy at the fact I'd been called in at all.

"Please tell me what you've learned so far. Mr. Valon told me there was an excellent crew working with the film."

Another smile. "We do have some experience. Well, it's as A. V. has probably told you, a total screwup. Rossol has been shooting some more film, but I think completion is doubtful. Of course, the official company position is that we're still hopeful."

"I see. And you've seen the film already."

"Well, all but this last batch. If all Dupres's work with Brook had been finished, it really would have been possible. But she has a Broadway show sched-

uled, and then, frankly, I don't know whom they'd
get to replace Brook for their scenes. A double, of
course, is out of the question. You realize none of
Brook's final close-ups had been done nor any of the
African sequence. Am I going too fast for you?''

"No, go ahead, please.''

"That's it, basically. I doubt very much anything
we'll see today will change my mind. Or yours."

"I'll want to see the footage that's here in the city
as well."

"Oh, that's a lot of film. Pam my secretary's prepared a complete synopsis, detailed down to the last
scene. I can get you a copy."

"Thanks."

"Here's the car. Bit of a tight squeeze. Shall I
drive?"

"If you like. But arrange for me to see the film in
any case."

He looked at me over the top of the car, then nodded. "Sure. Whatever you say. What branch are you
from?" he asked as he climbed into his seat.

"I'm attached to the home office."

"One of Mr. Valon's special people?"

"In a manner of speaking." I put on my sun-
glasses, as much against him as against the sudden
dazzling shafts that shot like klieg lights between the
tops of the high buildings. Ed, as he insisted I call
him, turned on the air-conditioning, and we rode with
its artificial whisper through the office canyons, up
the wide, dirty streets lined with beaten tenements and
idle men to the Byzantine maze of bridges, highways,
and overpasses that span the waterways and ware-
houses on the city's borders. To the sound of the traf-

fic, Ed added a complex stream of jargon and plati-
tudes, sufficient to conceal all but those most basic
human impulses, curiosity and suspicion. My brief
answers neither allayed nor discouraged him: his
chumminess was so persistent that it approached ag-
gression.

Finally we left the Taconic Parkway, and I had him
switch off the air conditioner and open the windows.
Early spring rushed through the car, bringing the
earthy smells of grass, manure, and cattle and inter-
rupting Ed's accounts of pictures past—had I worked
on that one?—and of weighty deals, satisfactory premiums, and actuarial coups. I concentrated on the rippling pastures, until the occasional gas stations and
roadside stands gave way to a proper collection of
houses and shops.

"This is the village," he announced. "Shall we
stop for lunch? We're not apt to get anything from
the film crew."

"Fine. I had an early start."

Ed parked in front of a small, white-pillared bank.
The village was a farm town going suburban, with
chic spreading like leprosy. There were a couple of
quaintly gotten-up antique stores and several shops
displaying crafts of dubious provenance. Only the
sturdy tractors and harrows still offered by the hardware store counteracted the general air of trendy striv-
ing.

"Looks like they're trying to smarten this place
up," said Ed.

During lunch at the diner, I asked about the cast
and wrote down the addresses of the missing actors,
an activity that puzzled him.

"There's no chance of their being assembled for reshooting," he said. "No chance at all. Sir Michael Burley's already in rehearsals for a very big BBC production, and Altheia Karl, she's the second female lead, reports for a film next week. It's impossible."

"Then Sir Michael is in London?"

"Well, no. It's one of those coproductions. The landing of the Pilgrims or the settling of the New World, or some such. He's Raleigh or Winthrop, one or the other, but I can't see what he has to do with our concerns now."

"I want to be able to get in touch with him—if it's necessary," I said, being deliberately mysterious.

When I added a pleasant smile, Ed stabbed the last of his apple pie and asked, "You done? After all, I've got to see those dailies and catch the late train."

"Whenever you're ready." I closed my notebook.

As we left he spoke testily. "It would be easier if I knew exactly how you were going to fit into the picture. I mean, there's no point in both of us watching the rushes and filing reports."

"Why not?"

"Simple duplication of effort. And this business is always a team operation. I think"—he lowered his voice confidentially—"between you and me, that another person coming on at this time is going to cause problems with our director. It's"—he flapped his hands like fins to indicate my destabilizing presence—"tricky."

"Too much money's at stake to worry about our film director's sensibilities," I said. "I should think you'd understand that."

In the first silence of the trip, Ed took us up the

state highway, through a hamlet consisting of a gas station, a restaurant, a public swimming pool, and a nursery, then, at an abrupt and rocky curve, turned into a long, sloping drive that led to an impressive plantation of hemlocks and spruce.

"The German forest sequences were shot here," he remarked.

Beyond the trees, an open lawn fronted a large, dark-wood chalet that was protected by ornamental gatehouses and a pair of solid wooden gates. Before these immense doors stood a handsome old Mercedes and, sitting smoking on the hood, an actor in a black SS uniform, sloppily opened over the chest to reveal his white T-shirt.

Ed slammed on the brakes and yelled for the doors to be opened, then pulled the car through into a large grassy courtyard. Two sides of this enclosure were occupied by the house, a fortresslike lower floor of round native fieldstone, surmounted by two more stories sheathed in dark shingles and capped with a steep roof broken by tiny attic dormers. The eaves were ornamented in fanciful gingerbread that matched the decorations on the stables and garages, which closed the other sides of the court. Whether or not this was authentically Bavarian in style, the effect of the sharply angled shadows on the court, the high, fanciful silhouette of the main building, the black line of conifers visible beyond the garage, and the bare courtyard floored in flagstones set in silky grayish grass were all appropriately strange and vaguely disquieting.

Ed went over to where the crew were drinking coffee beside a big Panavision Reflex. A large scrim was in place beside the camera, and it was obvious that a scene had been in progress that morning.

"Where's Len Rossol?"

One of the men, a grip, judging by his work clothes and powerful arms, jerked his chin toward the house, and Ed charged up the wide stone steps. Interested to see their meeting, I had started to follow, when the front door opened and a short, muscular man with a great deal of curly black hair and tinted aviator glasses stepped out onto the stoop. He was dressed in khaki pants and a plaid shirt, and only his general air of decisiveness and the expensive optical device dangling from the lanyard about his neck separated him from the rest of the crew.

"What are you working on?" Ed asked.

"Some stuff around the visit to Himmler. I want the best possible package for you."

"Take care of that antique Mercedes. Do you have to use that? Christ, they're expensive—you know any little scratch—"

"Keep your hair on, Ed. I'm doing my best for you. Worst comes to worst, I'll cut a documentary on the filming of *The Lazarus Gambit* and sell it as a tribute to Henry Brook. Your firm's got no imagination. Who's this?" he demanded, looking at me.

"I'm Anna Peters. The Independence Mutual home office asked me to look in."

"You brought a check?"

"I'm afraid not yet, Mr. Rossol."

"I don't want to talk to anyone without money. All right, guys, pack it up for today."

"The rushes," Ed said. "I've got to see the reels that haven't gone to the city. Listen, don't think In-

dependence Mutual doesn't appreciate your cooperation, but every bit of film means more work for me.''

Rossol gave a dry, unpleasant smile, clapped Ed on
the shoulder, and ran lightly down the steps to talk to
the crew. Then he jammed his hands into his pockets
and returned to the house, his shoulders hunched belligerently. "I need money," he announced in a loud
voice. "Can anyone take that message to the front
office? You," he said to me. "You tell them. Thanks
to that goddamn Henry Brook, I need money and I
need it now.''

There was an awkward, embarrassed silence.

"First, I think we need those dailies," I said.

Rossol ran his hand through his thick hair and returned to civilization. "Yeah. Be my guest. Upstairs.
I'm going to see the last rushes. You can have them
run the other stuff, too.''

"You know that the report can't go in officially
until we've seen everything, Len," Ed said. "All this
shooting and new scenes are appreciated but they
make complications. It's not my rule, it's company
policy.''

"Sure. Company policy takes my money the first
of every month, than hangs me out to dry when I need
cash. I'm not running a goddamn grocery store. I've
got a payroll every week and nothing coming in.''

"We're working just as fast as we can. That's why
Ms. Peters is here. Reinforcements," Ed said.

"Yeah," Rossol said and opened the door. He
waved him inside and gave me a sour, appraising
look. Like Ed, he did not seem totally pleased with
what he saw, for he said, "I goddamn sure don't need
any more aggravation.''

I sensed some not-so-casual anxiety beneath this casual rudeness, but before I could reply, a young woman with flying hair and an armload of papers rushed into the hallway. "Len, are you ready for the film?"

"Yeah. Gloria, honey, take care of these two. I'm not up to being ringmaster today." He waved vaguely in our direction. "Ed and—"

"Anna Peters. How are you?"

She shook my hand with the distracted air of the newly unemployed and led us upstairs to a long room with big windows and a cluster of upholstered and folding chairs facing a screen. "This was the ball-room," she said.

"Quite a place."

"It belongs to a friend of Len's." She smiled wistfully at the name, showing large, perfect teeth.

"What do you do?"

"I'm continuity." She saw this didn't register and tactfully whispered, "I keep a log of all scenes shot to make sure everything matches. If the ashtray is full or empty, if the performer looked left or right, every little detail."

"You must have an extraordinary memory," I said, putting her down as a possible source of information in spite of her somewhat flustered manner.

This brought a smile. "Len says I'm the best he's ever worked with. This will be—would have been, that is—our third picture together."

"So you worked on *Street Angel* and *Borodino?*"

"Yes, both."

"Terrific pictures," I said sincerely.

"You've seen them?"

"Yes, and my husband saw *Borodino* twice; he's an artist."

"It was the most beautiful film. Every frame is lovely. Len's a genius."

"And this one? Would this one have been as good, do you think?"

There was a moment too long, just one. "Some of the scenes were remarkable. When you see them, you'll agree." She pointed to a battered leather chair. "You can sit here. I'll go tell them to begin. Oh, and Ed, do you need anything?"

He shook his head but began to complain about her as soon as she left. "One of the most incompetent continuity girls I've ever worked with," he said in a whisper. "Sleeps with the director, of course. It's the way things are done."

The shutters were closed, and the April sun dwindled to thin glowing bars before these, too, were extinguished by heavy curtains.

"All right," Gloria called. With a whir the projector launched a shaft of light that resolved into a few numbers before the driveway to a chalet appeared on the screen, and the ancient Mercedes came over the brow of the hill, pennants with swastikas fluttering above the front fenders. The actor whom we'd seen as we arrived was driving, and Brook, or perhaps a double, sat in the rear, for there were no close-ups. Then came a variety of shots, including some through the windshield of the car, to introduce what appeared to be a formidable and forbidding edifice. Rossol had chosen angels to emphasize the eccentricity of the chalet, so that when Dr. Kleinz and his escort approached the main building they appeared to be walking beneath jagged teeth, and the car passed into the darkness of the gates as if entering a tunnel.

There was more footage, not of great interest, of German signs and of a roadside shrine erected along the drive to strengthen the impression of an Alpine roadway. At one point telephone lines appeared, and Rossol told Gloria to make a note to have that reshot. Otherwise, he was satisfied with his work and ordered the earlier dailies run.

The first sequence was the meeting with Himmler, which had been shot before the scenes of Kleinz's arrival. The SS driver led the professor into the hall downstairs, which, for the scene, had been furnished with a picture of the führer, swastikas, and SS insignia. This time the master shot, which Ed explained was the overall view of the action, was followed by different angles of the same scene and by a series of close-ups of the driver, of Kleinz, and of the servant who met them at the door. Despite the repetition, I was soon caught up like any other fan in imagining how the picture would have been assembled, as well as in the morbid fascination of watching the man whose accident I'd come to investigate. The knowledge that Brook had died only days after he paused in that hall to undo his scarf and give the servant his topcoat lent significance to each detail. But though I examined his face with the greatest care, Brook told me nothing. He had been completely immersed in his part. I could see only Dr. Kleinz's ambition and excitement, combined, because he was an intelligent man, with vague trepidation.

"The reichsführer will see you now."

A thin, cold-faced aide stood on the last step of the

stair. Kleinz followed him upstairs, past a variety of deer and boar heads and the disturbing counterpoint of the red-and-black swastikas. The next sequence opened with the interior of Himmler's study, showing the SS chief working at his desk. The camera looked over his shoulder at lists of figures, pausing long enough to permit the viewer to read *Dachau* and *Buchenwald*, then moving over a paperweight with the SS insignia and a small photograph of Himmler and the führer. At a knock on the door, Himmler looked up; his aide entered with a "Heil Hitler" to announce Dr. Kleinz.

"Professor Kleinz, what a pleasure to greet someone who is contributing such work to the fatherland."

"The members of my staff were most encouraged by your interest in our work, Herr Reichsführer."

The SS chief smiled. His voice was soft, his round face unlined. Only his eyes gave him away: rimmed by small steel glasses, they were intense and somehow impersonal. "I hope I will be able to give you further encouragement and assistance, Herr Professor. I have a genuine interest in the sciences, although my own degree was in agriculture."

"Of course, Herr Reichsführer."

When this sequence was repeated from Himmler's angle, I could see how subtly Brook was able to shade this reply. The perfect, almost obsequious politeness of his character was touched ever so delicately with the contempt that a man of Kleinz's background and education would feel for an ex-chicken farmer, however powerful. I also saw that those few lines represented Take 15 and thought I would have to ask Gloria—

"Could be of great assistance to the fatherland."
The light flashed on Himmler's glasses. "Whatever
can be done to save our brave fighting men—"

"I'm not clear, Herr Reichsführer, how we might
assist—"

"That will be left for us to decide. You would be
prepared to accept any orders." It was not a question.

The clock in the room ticked. "Of course," said
Dr. Kleinz.

"Your report mentioned the utility of this 'suspended animation' in difficult surgical cases and the
combination of the hormone with cold treatments."

"It is all still speculation. Trials in surgery would
depend on our success in synthesizing the hormone
in sufficient quantities."

"This must be done."

"Be assured, Herr Reichsführer, we will spare no
effort."

"I am sure you will not, Dr. Kleinz, when you
remember how many doctors are needed on the eastern front." In subsequent close-ups, the actor playing
Himmler had skillfully emphasized these words.
"Within six months? If every facility is made available?"

The camera panned to focus on Kleinz. The muscles tightened in his handsome face. "If we have everything we need."

"You will prepare a document outlining what is
necessary. It will be supplied."

"Thank you, Herr Reichsführer. Even then, you
understand, this would remain a highly experimental
process. We have tested it only on animals."

A close-up showed Himmler's smile and his glit-

tering eyes. "There is no lack of experimental sub-
jects. None whatsoever." His hands moved across to
the papers on his desk and the camera drew in to
show that he had been reading about concentration
camp allocations. The clock on the sideboard clicked
oppressively, and Kleinz looked as though he would
speak, he would ask; it was the crucial moment. Then
he nodded. "Of course, Herr Reichsführer." Twenty
takes had been required to secure that hesitation, that
surrender. Afterward, there were more close-ups and
an even tighter shot of the papers on Himmler's desk
before the two men were shown walking through a
pine forest where a little snow still touched the dead
leaves. Then the screen went white and someone
jumped up to open a curtain.

"We've got some footage of the last scene between
Lani and Henry. You want to run that, too?" the projectionist asked.

Ed looked at his watch. "How long is it? I'm trying
to catch a train."

"We'll just run the masters, if you like."

"Let's see the footage," I said. "You can go
ahead, Ed. I'll give you a report." There was some
discussion about this, but finally it was decided that
he would watch enough to be able to say he'd
checked the film, then hitch a ride into town with one
of the grips. The curtains closed, and more high take
numbers came up on the screen, surprising me again
with the vast amount of time consumed in shooting.
This sequence showed the interior of what Gloria
whispered was Hanna's apartment. "They were going
to cut in shots of Brook arriving later and some footage of Kiel to orient the scene."

A young woman with light brown hair and fine dark eyes was working at the stove in a small, dingy kitchen. Although pretty, she was plainly dressed and looked thin and tired. The close-up of her hands showed they were red, her nails short. The woman brushed the hair out of her eyes, glanced at her watch, then returned to work. She seemed full of nervous anticipation, and when the doorbell rang, she dropped her spoon and hurried to answer, pausing for an instant by the mirror to check her hair. These simple actions apparently represented a technically complex sequence, because there had been a lot of film shot and quite a number of different camera placements.

"Fancy stuff," Ed muttered and pushed the button that lit the dial of his watch.

"I'm coming," Hanna called when the bell sounded again.

She opened the door and threw her arms around Kleinz, then drew him inside, helping with his coat and scarf. Rossol had demanded twelve takes before he was satisfied with the business with the coat and with Kleinz's awkward presentation of a doll in Bavarian folk dress. There were shots of this gift being placed on a chest of drawers and close-ups of Hanna's radiant face and of Kleinz's more complex and ambiguous expressions. The couple embraced affectionately, but Hanna interrupted the professor's kisses to ask how the meeting had gone.

Kleinz teased her about this concern and asked her to bring out some wine. Everything would be all right, he assured her. The reichsführer was supporting his research and had ordered work on the synthetic hormone to proceed.

"It means you are working for them." Hanna's flat voice held a hint of accusation.

"It is for the fatherland," he said, but his hand trembled when he raised his glass. Then colder, "You don't understand what I'm doing." He lit a cigarette, the blue smoke dividing them like a curtain, and walked to the window. The camera saw him silhouetted against the pale evening light, then turned to follow Hanna's final preparations for the meal. Some close shots of her hands laying out a dainty salad contrasted the care and affection of her cookery with the now tense and sour mood of their meeting.

When she set a platter of stew down on the table, Hanna remained bent over the dish, her back stiff with anger and fear. "They've arrested Stefan," she said softly.

"Stefan?" Kleinz was astonished.

"Maria told me. They came to the lab. Those same SS that are going to support your research. They came and took him away."

"It is a mistake," Kleinz said with more assurance. "Everything was in order. His father was Polish but not a Jew. There should be no difficulty. We will call—"

Hanna straightened up, her face drained. "They will tell Maria nothing. He is gone and he is not the first. Have the others come back?"

"Jewish professors and students were removed by the decree—you knew that."

"And now the others. What will they accuse you of, Dieter? What will they say against us?"

"I have just spoken to the reichsführer himself. Our work is of the first importance."

"They have taken away our friend but you will work for them?"

"I will work for our country—for discoveries that will save lives."

Hanna looked down in despair. "You work only for yourself," she said.

Close-ups repeated this exchange. Brook's tight features shaded from arrogance to fear, and tears appeared in Hanna's eyes. Then the sequence ended, the curtains were opened, and the crew stood up and stretched. I asked Gloria if Lani Dupres was still around.

"She's leaving early tomorrow but I think she's in her room now. I'll take you up. Weren't the rushes marvelous?"

"Very impressive. But there seemed to be an awful lot of takes. Is that usual?"

"Well, Len is always careful and Brook is—was—a perfectionist."

"Was that how the production fell behind schedule?"

"Behind?" She stopped on the stair so abruptly that I nearly stepped on her heels.

"At least several weeks by our calculations."

"Oh, not that long! We were delayed a couple of days here because the warm weather meant the snow machine wouldn't work. It was in the seventies. That's why we were outdoors at the party where Henry—" She broke off and straightened her notebooks. "Len is always very professional. He always expects to bring his productions in on time. There's been some misunderstanding."

I left it at that. When we reached the top floor, she

knocked on a door tucked under the eaves. "Lani? It's Gloria. Someone to see you."

There were footsteps on the other side, and with a nervous smile Gloria nodded and hurried away.

THREE

"YES?" Lani Dupres opened the door and looked at me, then turned to see where Gloria had gone. "Gloria? That's just like her. If you're more local press, forget it." The long fingernails tapping irritably against the door were just one change from her portrait of Hanna. Although she was still pretty offscreen, Dupres looked smaller, darker, and very much sharper. She had abandoned the forties page boy for a sensible bun that emphasized the fine, clean lines of her face, and Hanna's genteelly shabby dress had been replaced by a pair of jeans and a dancer's leotard that showed there were no extra ounces on her slim frame. After a screen impersonation of long-suffering gentleness, the real Lani Dupres came as something of a surprise.

I opened my wallet for one of the Independence Mutual cards that Valon had supplied. "I've been asked to have a look at some of the film and to talk with the cast."

She glanced indifferently at my name and asked, "What for? I thought that Martins fellow was handling everything."

"Independence Mutual is a large company; insurance for the film and for the members of the cast were handled by several different departments. It's all routine. May I talk to you for a few minutes?"

"You've already started, haven't you?" But she

stepped aside to let me into the room. Although the ceiling was rather low and the furnishings spartan, the effect was a not unpleasant simplicity thanks to the fine view of the woods and fields beyond the house. She sat on the bed, and I took a straight chair by the writing table.

"This seems appropriate for Hanna," I remarked.

"Ex-servant's quarters. But I guess you're right. She'd be the patient Griselda type."

"Not your cup of tea, normally?"

"Not on your life."

"Still, you were very convincing. I saw some of your work just now."

"That last scene with Henry, you mean?"

"That's right. The dinner scene."

"'You will work only for yourself!'" she exclaimed; her face froze in grief and tears actually came into her eyes.

I found this disconcerting and said so.

Lani Dupres burst out laughing. "Henry was always jealous that I could cry on demand. That was the one thing he could never manage."

"Very impressive. Was this your first screen role?"

"First of any moment. Let's see, I was a cult member in a little Canadian production, and I had a bit part in *Quest for the Stars*."

"The big space drama?"

"Yes, as a slave girl from a satellite of Alpha Centauri. This was something else. And, of course, to work with Brook and Rossol in one's first starring role"—she gestured expansively, creating a dramatic pause that made me think she had not found the attentions of the local press quite as oppressive as she'd suggested—"it was marvelous. Simply marvelous."

"The accident must have come as a great shock—and a great professional disappointment."

"Oh, yes." She was self-consciously tragic. "We were all devastated. Simply devastated. I wept for days, but it was such an honor to have performed with him in his last role."

I found it curious that someone capable of such subtlety on the screen should seem so theatrical, even affected, offstage.

"Some of the cast hope the picture can be finished or changed," she continued, "but I know that Brook can't be replaced. The picture would have been a masterpiece. The chemistry on the set was indescribable."

"I see." What I saw was that Lani Dupres had cleverly cast herself in one legendary picture that would never have to face the critics. "But it could have been salvaged, couldn't it, if the production had been strictly on schedule?"

"What do you mean?"

"Well, Ms. Dupres, from what Independence Mutual has figured, the production was at least several weeks behind. In fact, I believe the company had been scheduled to leave this location ten days or so before Henry Brook's accident."

"It was his karma," she said dramatically. She picked up her cigarettes, shook one out, then extended the pack.

"No, thanks, I gave it up."

"Lucky you. I'm going to quit before I start *Vaudeville Babes*." Although she drew greedily on the cigarette, I believed her. She seemed thoroughly professional.

"What did you mean about Brook?"

"Well, it was his fault if we were behind—his and the warm weather. That was unexpected."

"How his fault?"

She sighed, exhaling a smoky cloud. "He was brilliant. The most brilliant man I've ever worked with." There was another pause while the twenty-one-year-old studied the end of her cigarette as though she'd the experience of a Duse. "But moody," she added. "He was a great, instinctive performer. Everything was temperament."

"And he was difficult to work with?"

"No, no. At least not for me. It was a joy, a challenge. The set was electric, but—"

I waited.

"—not conducive to exact scheduling." She gave a little wave of her hand as if great artists could not be troubled with such things.

"How did the rest of the cast react to him?"

But now Dupres turned cautious. "I really don't see what that has to do with the insurance company."

"I'm trying to determine what Brook was like. What his state of mind might have been."

"Oh." This seemed a new thought. "I assumed everything was settled. It was just an accident. It could have happened to any one of us. You know parties."

"Unfortunately, it happened to the one person who was irreplaceable—at least on this production. Naturally, we'd like to know a little more about him."

"Like what?" Her voice was quick and sharp but interested, too.

"You say he was moody, temperamental. Was he upset about something or depressed?"

Lani Dupres laughed. "No. He was an old-timer. Very capable. He's always been temperamental. This time"—she shrugged—"the chemistry was extraordinary, that's all I can tell you." Then her theatrical sense enveloped her. "If there was any conflict, it was producing wonderful, exciting work. You've seen the rushes. Would any actor leave that?"

"It doesn't seem likely, but why were so many takes required to get results?"

"Actually, that was true only with Brook. The rest of our work went rather more quickly."

Interesting. "And Mr. Rossol—didn't these delays disturb him?"

"He got what he wanted," Lani Dupres said. "From all of us, don't you think?"

"It seems so," I admitted.

When she smiled, she resembled her image on the screen, but she immediately stood up, rubbing out her cigarette in the ashtray by the bed. "I'm sorry, but I really must pack. I leave tomorrow."

"Your work was not quite complete, was it?"

"Not quite. I had some close-ups to be shot in the studio and the reunification scene."

"What was that?"

"Oh, the SS heavies get onto Kleinz to leave Hanna. She's considered politically unreliable, and finally he breaks with her. 'You're choosing death. I can smell it on you!'" She raised her hand to her mouth, then her expression relaxed. "It was to have ended on a very long, almost freeze-frame close-up of me, damn it. It would have been a real career breakthrough. And my final scenes in the camp—oh, yes, poor Hanna comes to a bad end—I would have been simply shattering."

She had a regretful, faraway air, and I knew that I would not learn any more about Henry Brook at the moment.

"You've been very helpful. If I could have your New York address just in case there's some question. I'm not sure whether there's any chance of further compensation for the cast..."

"Oh well, if there's any cash, do see I get it," she said, scribbling a line. "I'll be at the theater—at the Belasco—starting in two weeks."

"Good luck, Ms. Dupres."

"Thank you." She held open the door.

I paused on the threshold. "Was Henry Brook a likable man?"

But Lani Dupres was not so easily caught off guard. "Henry Brook," she said firmly, "was a great artist."

Her door closed, my feet clattered on the bare steps, then, at the second floor landing, silence. The movie people had left the ballroom for the warren of rooms in the house or had gone to set up their cameras again. Probably the latter, for I suspected that Rossol's nerves did not permit him to sit idle. A walk along the corridors on the lower floors revealed no one about, and I went across to the room over the garage, where my case had been deposited, to change into a pair of corduroy slacks, a windbreaker, and walking shoes. Taking my binoculars and car keys, I went downstairs to phone my office.

"Baby?"

"Hello, Anna. You up in New York?"

"I'm farther than that. On scenic location. Don't call me here, I'll ring you tomorrow night."

"Sure. What do you want?"

"I want some information on the financial condition of Leonard Rossol's film company, New Biograph."

"That's it?"

"For now."

"You meeting all the stars?" Baby inquired. June Quigley, aka Baby, has a taste for glitz and a great head for figures.

"Some of them anyway. See if you can have that by tomorrow night."

She agreed to try, and I pulled on my coat and went outside. One of the crew was sitting on the step blowing wheezy chords on a harmonica. "Leaving?" he asked.

"Not yet. I thought I'd see some of the countryside."

He noticed the binoculars. "Lots of nice birds around. Big ones. But don't go into the fields here."

"Why not?"

"They keep elk. Mean bastards."

"Thanks, I won't forget."

"Some life, huh?"

"Yeah. By the way, where do you eat around here?"

"Lunch is brought in from town. Dinners we have two sittings at the biggest local restaurant, The Huntsman. You'll get a meal there if you mention you're attached to the film.''

"Good. What time?"

"Grips and technical crew usually go in around five-thirty; director and cast at six-fifteen. Otherwise we'd swamp the place."

"I'll see you then." I maneuvered my car gingerly through the gates, then paused at the foot of the drive to check the map and Valon's directions. The second location was about six miles away on the other side of the village, and it turned out to be hard to miss, what with the two big stone towers flanking a twelve-foot iron gate at the entrance. That was for starters. Beyond the barrier, which, fortunately, had been left open, was a lake bordered by hemlocks, which I was later to recognize in an outdoor scene between Brook and Lani Dupres. Next came an impressive group of fieldstone barns and stables, a rustic hunting lodge that was shut up tight, and, finally, around the far side of the water, a Victorian chateau with a formal garden. I parked on the gravel drive at the rear and tried both the front and back doors without success. A glance through the windows told me that the place was furnished and lived in, though deserted at the moment. There would undoubtedly be a caretaker, but feeling that I had done as much as courtesy required, I took the opportunity to have a quiet look around on my own.

From the front terrace, a flagstone path led across a neat lawn bordered with neglected perennials. Below lay a rose garden, also in need of attention, and beyond a hedge of rhododendrons and azaleas, an English garden that merged into the fields and seemed

to be surviving nicely. The history of this place, I
thought, must be interesting, for the vast and eccentric
estate showed some marked shifts in taste. The outbuildings and the planted forest were clearly of
German inspiration, but someone—wife, son, daugh-
ter, heir—had tired of that Nordic gloom and demanded not only the opulent stone house behind me
but also these sunny gardens and the open stretch of
oaks, maples, and flowering shrubs that ran down to
the water. The wide and handsome sweep gave an
impression of exuberant fertility, a feeling strengthened by the calls of peepers from the low places beyond the trees, the sounds of the crows, sparrows, and
redwings, and, under their songs, the soft hiss of water draining into thawed earth. With this sibilant ac-
companiment, I picked my way through the long,
damp grass to the summerhouse by the edge of the
water. All but hidden from the main house by trees
and the hill, this large pavilion was where the film
company had held the fatal party.

The door was locked, but through the arched windows, I could see a few trestle tables lined up inside,
along with cartons of empty champagne bottles and a
few sad paper streamers. Past a narrow strip of grass
and myrtle, a raised boardwalk led along the water to
a boathouse and then out at an angle to form a dock.
I sat on the top step to consult the handful of clippings
about Brook's accident that I'd stuck in my notebook
along with the sequence of events. The information
seemed straightforward and, as news reports go, remarkably consistent. The company of *The Lazarus
Gambit* had thrown a party near the end of their location shooting, when the unseasonably warm

weather permitted use of the summerhouse. The party
had begun with a supper and continued with dancing
and merriment until well after midnight. There had
been a good deal of revelry and a great deal of noise,
and anyone who had noticed Brook's absence assumed he had returned to his room. Times when the
cast had last seen him varied considerably. Some said
he had definitely been there around ten-thirty. Others
put it closer to midnight or even after. In any case,
Brook had apparently walked onto the jetty, probably
to the end near the boathouse, fallen into the water,
and, unable to attract attention over the amplified music, drowned.

I returned the clips to my notebook, then walked
around the summerhouse. The movie people had been
neat and careful. The only signs of their presence that
I could detect were some new U nails remaining in
the wood trim over the doors and some larger ones
left in the jetty. With lights and music, the pavilion
would have created a pretty effect, a little Hollywood
glamour to cheer the cast after their long exile, to
entertain the locals, and to thank the owner of this
remarkable estate.

The cold breeze put a soft little ripple on the lake,
and I began idly dropping stray bits of gravel into the
water. Murky and green with pond weeds near the
bank, the lake seemed surprisingly shallow, and, curious, I took out a piece of string, tied a small stone
on the end, and made a trial. The water level dropped
from three feet immediately at the shore to only about
a foot more halfway out. Clearly Brook hadn't taken
a tumble there. I walked to the end, knelt down on
the bleached, splintery boards, and again lowered the

string. It sank into the dark water, disturbing a feathery mat of weeds before touching the soft bottom. I pulled it up, standing to measure the depth. The wet mark on the string was no more than five and a half feet. I could almost have stood on the bottom and still managed to breathe. Was that right? I tried again, then tested the water at the other corner of the jetty and all along the other side. The maximum depth was still less than my by no means unusual height. Unless Brook had performed during his entire career standing on a box, he was at least my size and should have been able to touch bottom.

There were explanations, of course. He might have been very drunk, although the coroner had denied that. There would be a blood report, surely, which would settle the question. He might have struck his head. There was a scuff reported on his face but no skull injuries. A combination, perhaps, of mild tipsiness and a fall? Panic? It was not inconceivable. On the other hand, Valon's suspicion of suicide was not ruled out. It would have taken obvious desperation to drown oneself directly by the jetty, but for a swimmer, there were other possibilities; the water was frigid, the lake wide. It might not take very long for a man to lose consciousness nor a great distance before the water was over his head, a scenario that seemed to me more probable than a fatal slip into the cold but shallow water near the dock.

I pulled up the string and walked back down the jetty. I didn't like this place and stopped to think why not. Perhaps it was the dark pines looming up on the other sides of the lake. Or just the cold air stirring over the water, noticeable after the heat of D.C. I

thought of the conversation I'd had a couple of weeks
before with a psychic who had been in the capital on
a missing persons case. I'd been skeptical, but she
had a good record and her method was intriguing. She
always insisted on visiting the location of the crime
if it was a murder case or on having some of the
missing person's possessions, her theory being that
actions left traces just as physical bodies do. That was
clearly just this side of mumbo jumbo, but as I
watched the cold shadows advancing from the
"German forest," I couldn't help wondering what she
would have made of the place where Henry Brook
died. The newspaper reports and Valon's information
had given me one impression. Standing on the jetty
over the dark, weedy lake gave me quite a different
one; something was wrong. Valon might be right,
or—But I didn't get to finish this thought, because
there was a great barking from the vicinity of the
boathouse, and three dogs came into sight, a brown-
and-white spaniel, a little buff terrier, and an immense
and belligerent bull mastiff. Their nails rattled over
the boards, and then about five yards away, the big
dog stopped and barked twice. The smaller ones approached, jumping and slobbering, willing to be
friendly, but when I took a step forward, the mastiff
lowered its heavy head and growled.

"Hector! Hector!"

The big animal barked in response and, considerably relieved, I called, "Hello."

Around the hedge by the boathouse a small, slight
man in hunting clothes appeared with a leash in his
hand and a .22 rifle on his shoulder. His tanned, an-
gular face was seamed by age and hard winters. He

whistled, and the spaniel and the terrier ran back wagging their tails, but although Hector looked over his shoulder till he showed the whites of his eyes, the big dog never budged.

"Ahhh, damn stubborn pup," the man said in a soft burr and walked up briskly to snap on the leash. "Well," he said, "I expect you've been seeing where it happened."

I produced a card, passing it cautiously over the dog. "I rang the bell at the house but got no answer."

"I saw where you'd left your car." He read the card carefully before putting it in his pocket. "I was off shooting rats about the stables. If they'll not have some cats, they must expect vermin."

"There's no farm at all?"

"No, no. No interest. It's a summer place now. Was opened special for the movie folk. Fine lot of good it did them."

"Yes. I'm sorry to have disturbed you, Mr.—"

"McNab. Had you called, I would have showed you round."

"It was rather sudden. I was only told to come up here yesterday."

"The old story," he said, not unsympathetically. He gave the dog a pat. "You're not feared of dogs?"

"Not usually."

He unfastened the leash. "He'll not trouble you now, seeing I'm talking to you. Strangers he's taught to hold till I come."

"He looks very capable."

"Aye, a good beast." He had lowered his rifle, too, and now fished a pipe and his tobacco from a pocket. During this operation, I tried to guess his precise status. Was he an old member of the staff, knowl-edgeable but discreet, or was he someone new, talk-ative but uninformed?

"You must be the caretaker," I said when the pipe was lit.

"These past three years. Winters, anyway. When they come up in the summer they bring a staff."

"They'd need to. It's an enormous place."

"It was a showplace once. Now they don't bother themselves."

"The film company shot here a couple of weeks ago, am I right?"

"Yes," he said, drawing slowly on his pipe. "They're friends of young Mr. Delf's. Not people his parents would know." There was a definite hint of Old World disapproval: actors and theater people were suspect, and, of course, they had lived up to their reputations in a spectacular way.

"Is Mr. Delf here now?"

The caretaker shook his head. "Not since the ac-cident. A great upset. And a lot of work for me, I can tell you."

"Why did they have the party down here?"

"To save the house. There's no one in staff. No one at all. I'm not supposed to have to do anything but check the water and the furnace and keep an eye on who's about. Course for the party, I obliged, you understand."

I nodded. The big dog nudged the caretaker as if eager to resume his patrol, but his master ignored the hint. The arrival of the movie people had been an event, a troublesome but lively interruption after the long, silent country winter. The disaster would have been a topic in the small village beyond the gates, and I suspected my informant was not yet tired of rehearsing his part in those sensational events.

"Run the electric line down here."

I looked as surprised as possible.

"A great fuss. They brought all the liquor and food in with a truck. Long way around, of course. I said Mrs. Delf would never stand for the lawn being dug up, and I said that to young Mr. Delf as well, though he didn't like it."

I imagined Delf as the theater-struck son of comfortable, conservative wealth and guessed McNab was right.

"And they would have lights. All white. Sent back a string of colored ones as not the right effect."

"Quite a production."

"Right you are. That director fellow knows his stuff, though. Him and one of the electricians put up lights out here. They carry their own workmen, you know."

"Yes, so I'm told."

"Still, Rossol, that was his name, could do most of what needed doing himself—wiring, hammering, decorating. I couldn't believe the fuss—not to mention the liquor. And everything to be taken down the next morning. I couldn't see the point. But they didn't have to worry about that. Bright and early, me and Jim Gibb from over at Larches' place came to start pulling everything apart."

"What about the film crew's cables and stuff?"

"They were to come for them later, themselves, but of course, there was a bit of excitement by that time." He nodded for emphasis and resumed his narrative.

"Jim and me get to the end of the jetty. Right here,"
he said and strode to the edge of the dock. "We were
just taking down the nails on the last of the light
supports when Jim looks over the side and says,
'Mother of God!' and I look down and there he was,
floating like a dead fish."

FOUR

Mr. McNab was a country man with diverse skills and garrulous habits; by the time I left, I had not only a pretty good idea of events surrounding the party but also enlightenment on the proper care for neglected roses, the temperament of mastiffs, and sundry other topics suggested by our leisurely return from the summerhouse. Since it was already after six-thirty, I drove immediately to The Huntsman, a restaurant belonging to the family of Italian-plus-steak outfits and marked like all its ilk with dark wood paneling, red linens, and low lighting. The technical staff had already departed, but the director and most of the cast were still working through dessert and smoking up a storm.

Rossol was holding court at one end of a long table. He was still dressed in his faded work shirt and pants, but he had added a line of gold jewelry and a fringed western jacket. With Gloria on his left and Lani Dupres on his right, he seemed in much better humor, laughing and joking with the two women until I approached with the waiter. Rossol's face darkened when he saw us; then, doubtless remembering the vast funds that an Independence Mutual representative might command, he greeted me in a loud, expansive manner, insisting everyone make room at the head of the table for "another charming addition." There was a general shuffling of plates and places before he introduced me to the group as "our possible salvation," and asked again when his money would be forthcoming.

"I'm afraid that's Ed Martins's department."

"We're lost," he said in a dramatic whisper. "Lost. Lost."

"It's a corporate decision, Mr. Rossol. If everything is in order, there is no reason why you shouldn't be compensated."

"'Had we but world enough and time, this coyness, Lady, were no crime....'" When he smiled, Rossol lacked only subtlety to be a most attractive man, but he was clearly used to easy conquests. The present setup was fairly easy to read, even with half an eye on The Huntsman's menu, for Gloria was watching him with uneasy adoration on one side, while on the other, Lani was toying with her ice cream, her expression revealing the sly amusement of a clever woman about to let a man make a fool of himself for her benefit. Feeling that a third admirer would be superfluous, I decided to squelch the little ripple of laughter that ran around the table. "Henry Brook has already provided intimations of mortality," I said.

Rossol shifted gears instantly. "Poor Henry. You must excuse us; we are still not ourselves. You'd seen his work?" He leaned forward and rested his elbows on the table as though deeply interested in my present—and possibly future—opinions.

"Yes, almost everything he ever made. He was a marvelous performer."

"More than that. You may know insurance and corporate policy; I know actors. Henry was a genius. I don't say that lightly." He leaned back, brushing away the smoke from his cigar, for he was always producing little bits of theatrical business as though some invisible camera were grinding on, unseen, beyond his chair. "Everyone's a 'genius' in the movies, but Henry was the real thing."

I nodded.

"No one else could have played Kleinz. No one. That's been suggested. Did you know that?"

"What?"

"That we reshoot everything Henry did. Replace Lani if necessary—sorry, darling," he said to her, "you understand it's not my idea—and just save the scenes where Kleinz was absent."

"Is that possible?" I asked, rather dubious.

"No, it's not possible," he said, setting his glass down so hard that some wine slopped onto the cloth. "Possible maybe to recut and edit around Henry. I've explained that to your corporate people, and I've been working my ass off trying to do that. But to redo it with another actor? Never! If I'd thought someone else could have done the role, I'd have hired him originally. This wasn't some package; I had control all the way, and Brook had everything. He was a star who could act. They're one in a million. Am I right, Gloria?" He draped his arm across the back of her chair.

"Oh yes, and with the right director..." She gave a little smile as if on cue, and Rossol showed his expensive dentistry.

"It was a very difficult role," he continued. "Very difficult." He tipped his chair forward again and tapped his cigar thoughtfully against the ashtray.

"I suppose it depended on what you wanted to do with the role and with the book," I said. "*The Laz-*

arus Gambit is rather different from your earlier material, isn't it?''

"Because the book was a best-seller?"

"No, because it's entertaining but not very good."

Rossol became excited. "A second-rate book is no obstacle to a good movie. Let me explain: what matters for a film are the visual possibilities. How well the material can be conveyed in a visual manner. That's all. Fine writing...all that is extra from a filmmaker's point of view."

"Still, your earlier pictures—*Borodino* was an excellent novel. And weren't your other scripts your own?"

"That's true. And I've been accused of crass commercialism for picking up *The Lazarus Gambit,* which is funny, since most of my other pictures were financial successes."

"So I understand."

"And this one would have been too. I'm sure you see why."

"I'm afraid not at the moment, but I haven't finished reading—"

"It's the theme. That's what counts. Theme and characters. The sensational aspects, the melodrama—we accept those if the theme and the human values are good. Right?"

He looked around the table and everyone hastened to agree except me. "*The Lazarus Gambit* is a thriller that throws in everything but the atom bomb and the kitchen sink," I said.

"Ignore that. It's about guilt and redemption—a classic situation. A man does an evil thing—or, more exactly, involves himself with an evil thing, in this case not out of positive wickedness but out of moral anesthesia."

"They amount to the same thing for the victims."

"We're talking now about personality, about the effects on the individual. Albert Speer acquiesced to evil, but he was not a Bormann, not a Himmler. He had possibilities that were not awakened in time, but which were there nonetheless. The others lacked any ethical nature."

"And you see Kleinz as a Speer?"

"As that sort of man, yes. Brook and I talked a great deal about it. He did a lot of research for his characters."

"Speer was a friend of Hitler's, wasn't he? A personal friend?"

"Yes, and he was fascinated by him. Absolutely and fatally mesmerized."

"Kleinz hasn't that excuse. No one was fascinated by Himmler—" I suddenly realized that the round-faced, nondescript man across from me was the actor who had impersonated the reichsführer so chillingly. "Although you were very good. It was you, wasn't it?"

"Yes. With much thanks to the makeup department."

"It's really strange. I'd always believed performers looked pretty much the same offscreen."

They all laughed at this, and the conversation might have gone off in any number of directions if Rossol hadn't immediately picked up the thread of the argument. "Kleinz," he said sharply, "is Faust. He is not liable to personal fascinations. What he wants is knowledge."

"Yet he forsakes theoretical knowledge," Lani protested. "He betrays that—that's why the second quarrel scene is crucial."

"Agreed, agreed. It's out of fear. Do you think it's fear?" he asked the table at large. "I think it's fear, but Henry insisted it was vanity, ambition. What do you think?" He fixed his large, dark eyes on me as though he expected some revelation or surprise—or future advantage.

"I can't tell yet. There's nothing harder to judge than motivation."

"How fortunate that you never have to. You don't, do you? It's all statistics with insurance. You can deal in probability."

"I should have thought actors did too. The plausible will do, won't it?"

There was some debate about this. "Himmler," a careful craftsman, felt this was sufficient. Dupres disagreed, and Rossol came down somewhere in the middle, as befitted a director who had to work with actors of many different styles and persuasions.

"Either way," he said finally, "Kleinz is a man of our time. His private interests and obsessions involve him in larger evils. He assents to the state as we all do. No, no," Rossol said when the others disagreed. "A few marches, petitions, letters on the Kurds or El Salvador—what are those in the context of our submission and dependence? Modern life for the masses requires an assent, a participation in the state."

"Not everyone experiments on people in concentration camps," protested one of the cast.

"No, but that's emblematic. Film is exaggerated and emblematic. That's why it is the premier art form of our time: the very exaggerations are crucial. No, degree is not the point. The point is, how can a man be saved afterward? Saved from a disastrous assent to the state?''

"In what way?'' I asked, genuinely curious.

"Saved, redeemed,'' Rossol said.

"The somewhat melodramatic plot gives him the chance to do something socially useful. Is that salvation?''

"There's nothing else,'' Rossol said. "What else is there? Some sort of spiritual redemption without evidence?''

"Faith without works is suspect these days,'' "Himmler'' said and winked.

"Well, what else is there?'' Rossol demanded.

"I don't know. It seems to me that in the book's context, Kleinz does appalling things to further his career, then, if I have the story right, does one thing that will attack or prevent future evils. Socially, I guess that's useful. That's good. I'm just not sure it's sufficient.''

"Sufficient? He prevents the resurgence of Nazism—''

"She means he acts only within the political, the social framework,'' Lani Dupres said.

"That's good enough as far as I'm concerned,'' Rossol said.

"Well, then, is Kleinz a good man in the end?''

"He's dead at the end,'' said Gloria.

"An apocalyptic redemption,'' Rossol said. "A hopeful Götterdämmerung. Kleinz has a chance, not to undo his work, but to keep evil men from using his discoveries to further their own ends. He acts against evil and saves himself.''

"And civilization," "Himmler" said dryly.

"Yes, yes, an exaggeration," Rossol admitted, "but the plot is only the armature. The framework. For the popular audience, one needs something fairly graphic. I don't mean to sound contemptuous; all pictures require spectacle, and by the same token, you can get away with things in visuals that wouldn't work in print. *The Lazarus Gambit* suggested spectacular possibilities." He held up his hands as if framing a scene and shook his head. "Some of the best didn't get shot."

"Berlin was wonderful, though," Gloria said quickly. "The Berlin in flames sequence was really brilliant."

"All studio work. How I love studio work. I love the control. And for the climax—for the climax of the picture, I had such plans." He rubbed out his little green cigar and immediately lit another, which he proceeded to ignore as he had the first. "I had a chance to capture the nightmare of our time. Oh, Coppola's first part of *Apocalypse Now* is almost untouchable, but he didn't have plot. Couldn't end it—the big scenes came too early, so it lost impact. There was a chance with this—melodrama and all. And you see we had the character. Kleinz was absolutely right."

"And Brook was right for him?"

"There was no one else. *The Lazarus Gambit* will never be made. At least, not by me. What's left is a monument to Henry Brook." He raised his glass. "To Henry," he said solemnly. Then he stood up and the little coterie about him began pushing back their chairs and gathering their coats.

"We'll see you in New York?"

"I'll be in to see the film," I promised.

"You will see a great performance and a very great actor." With this, Rossol nodded rapidly and, without waiting for his companions, strode out of the restaurant, leaving me sitting across the table from "Heinrich Himmler," who of all the cast had decided neither to exit with the director nor head for the lounge.

There was a pause in which he lit a cigarette, and I ordered a piece of pie. Then I said, "I'm sorry, I didn't catch your name. I can't keep thinking of you as Herr Reichsführer."

"No, please don't. Alfred Hauer. That looks good," he added when the waiter brought my dessert. "I'll have one too, please, and another cup of coffee."

"Another pie," the waiter said, writing on his pad. "Blueberry, okay?"

"Please."

"It's very good," I told him.

"Homemade," the waiter said. "My sister bakes."

"Lucky I'm leaving. I should be dieting already, losing Himmler for my new role. Here I am stuck with guilt, fat, and no credit."

"It is too bad. I thought you were very good, Mr. Hauer."

"Bless you. Call me Alfie. My mother disapproved, though," he remarked as his order came. "Didn't think it suitable at all. First thing she said when I called with the bad news was 'Thank God, now you can get a respectable part.'" He said this in a properly lugubrious tone, but his light eyes were amused.

"Poor mother. And have you landed a respectable role?"

"Oh, yes. Or rather, no. I'm to play a doctor. Off Broadway."

"That sounds good—from a mother's point of view."

"Excellent. But he's a homicidal maniac in a rather black comedy."

"No Ladies' Circle Matinee?"

"That will depend entirely on the profits. If it and I are an immense success, all will be forgiven."

"Good luck."

"Thank you. I start next week."

"Are you basically a stage actor?"

"Yes, although I do an occasional character part in the movies to pay the rent." He had finished the last crumb of his pie and now began to look longingly at the crust of mine. "I believe I might have another piece. Nerves," he said complacently, like a man who will take his excuses where he can find them. He waved and held up two fingers to the waiter, who, used to his habits, appeared with a refill.

"Was it difficult acting with the movie people like Brook?"

"About as you'd imagine," he replied, discreet and evasive.

"I haven't much imagination where movie stars are concerned. What sort of man was Brook?"

"Henry? Henry was a son of a bitch."

"That's something I can imagine."

"Well, let your imagination run, because he was

one of a kind. But don't quote me. For public consumption, he was a genius and a pillar of the industry.''

"I've heard that before. Just how did his character show up?''

At this, Alfie left his pie and leaned back in his chair to look at me thoughtfully. "You seem very concerned with Henry Brook. Why? What's your interest?''

"Part of my job.''

He shook his head. "That's not the way Ed Martins goes about his business.''

"True.''

"And even allowing for the peculiarities of Ed's personality…'' There was a pause after which at least partial honesty seemed required.

"I'm with another division. We have a personal policy on Brook. Rather a large one.''

Alfie gave a short, cynical laugh. "And you want to get out of paying up?''

"The company would like to know for sure.''

"Like Big Brother.''

"Very like,'' I said easily, "but considerably more discreet.''

"Well, you can rule out suicide and pay up.''

"Oh?'' I was interested that he was so quick, so positive.

"Sure. If Henry Brook had killed himself, he'd have gone out on a pyre with fireworks, professional mourners, and full network coverage.''

"Not the retiring type who'd have taken a swim on a dark night?''

"Not Henry. Definitely not. I say that, although I didn't know him well—but I knew him enough."

It was a distinction I understood.

"I suppose," he continued more philosophically, "his personality was the result of being a star—of being *the* Henry Brook with nonstop attention, adulation, and money."

"Those never seem to come to people who can tolerate them," I said.

He smiled but now he wasn't joking. "It's corrupting. Like power; well, it is power. They're all correct: on screen, he had magnetism, charisma, sex appeal, whatever. The camera loved him and he loved the camera."

"And in private life?"

"He had no private life. The retinue's gone. But they were all here." He finished his pie, then said, "You know why?"

I shook my head.

"To create a continual set, a continual theater. What was he offstage? I don't know. I'm not sure he did either."

"Not a man to be envied."

"No. Of course, with that type, they're giving the ulcers. They make the scenes, they show up late for shooting, they demand retakes and fluff lines, they have the crisis and want to take a break."

"And so pictures get behind."

Alfie nodded. "You know about that?"

"Just a little. The company keeps track of the schedule. Had things been on time, most of Brook's work would have been finished."

"It might, it might not."

"Why's that?"

"He was having problems. Not so much up here—I hadn't any big trouble working with him—but I understand things had been difficult in New York. Some sort of crisis. You must understand with Henry even fairly mundane problems called for big emotional scenes. His way of working himself up for a role, I suppose."

"One would have thought the opposite true with Kleinz—he's so cold and repressed."

"That's deceiving. You don't get that feeling on the screen. He's not a dead character but a very vivid one. A cold, passionate man."

"That's true."

"There you are. That was Henry's genius. When he was ready, when he finally got down to business, he was terrific. He really lived on the screen."

"How did he and Rossol get on? Your director seems a nervous man."

"Very tight, yes. But he was patient with Henry, at least when I worked with them. Shot around him when the great man was late, that sort of thing. I don't know about the rest of the time. It was a long picture."

"Did Brook drink? Or use anything else?"

Alfie shook his head. "No. Believe it or not, Brook was always cold sober."

"It pays to check," I said. Valon would be disappointed, but if nothing more than this turned up...? "Can I give you a ride back?"

"Thanks. Keep me from eating myself out of my new role."

I paid my bill and we left. Along the way, we

talked in a desultory manner about the curious village locations and about theater in D.C., where he had appeared on tour. But as we pulled into the moonlit courtyard, I asked about Brook's retinue.

"Probably they'll be in the city—or out on the Coast. Marylin is in New York, I know. I don't know where Belinda went."

"Who's Marylin and who's Belinda?"

"Marylin is his wife, or his ex, or almost ex—their exact legal status was a puzzle to me."

"Not the mother of his son?"

"No. The boy was two marriages ago. Marylin was his third wife and remained as a sort of additional business manager, although how that worked out with his agent..." He shrugged expressively. "Marylin Cheney Brook lives in Manhattan. Should be pretty easy to find."

"And Belinda?"

"Oh, Belinda. She may or may not be with Marylin. My guess is that she'll be back on the Coast, but call Brook's agent, Edson Delaine."

"All right, thanks. Just what was her relationship?"

"Underage playmate," Alfie said with an expression of distaste. "Little girl lost or baby predator, take your pick. Not the most wholesome young lady."

"Henry Brook seems to have led a full and interesting life."

"Indeed, he did." Alfie opened his door. "Thanks for the lift. Normally, I could offer you a few exciting hands of gin rummy, but I've got to study my lines."

"That's all right, I've got some homework of my own."

Alfie went up the steps of the main house, and I returned to my room above the garage. A few of the grips were having a serious card game down the hall, and a radio was playing country music of the "I've drunk, I've suffered" school, but the structure was well built. Once my door closed, the voices were muffled, and over the bare night fields the only sounds were an occasional car taking the sharp bend down on the highway and the thin, high yapping of a lonely fox. I stretched out on the bed and made notes of my conversation with Alfie before returning to Dr. Kleinz's experiments, which, with the bottomless coffers of the SS, were making rapid progress. I skimmed the quarrels with Hanna that had so inspired Lani Dupres and reached the doctor's envelopment by the Nazi technocrats that sealed his fate. His work was a brilliant triumph; the hormone was synthesized; the animal experiments proved a success. Kleinz sat in his laboratory at Kiel one night quietly toasting his victory and sketching a career full of honor and utility.

In the next chapter, he and all his equipment were moved to a new lab for the final tests on human "volunteers." At Dachau.

FIVE

THE GIRL DIED at midday. Willi had monitored her heartbeat and respiration since she was started on the intravenous solution containing the synthetic hormone around eight. All signs remained normal until the cooling process used to enhance the effects of the hormone was well advanced. Then, as her body temperature dropped past the crucial seventy-degree mark, her heart began fibrillating.

Willi penciled the notation on his chart, then shouted, "Herr Doktor! Herr Doktor Kleinz!"

Kleinz leapt up from his desk and raced along the corridor to the surgery.

"It is her heart, Herr Doktor."

"Shut down the cooling unit and cut off the IV," Kleinz ordered. From the table beside the cooling bath, he grabbed a syringe, splashed some alcohol on the girl's thin arm, and injected the stimulant.

"The heart is still erratic, Herr Doktor."

"Help me lift her up. Hurry! We must raise the temperature as quickly as possible. And get some blankets." The girl was laid naked and dripping on the surgical table, her waxy limbs festooned with a trail of tubing like seaweed....

"TICKETS, tickets, please."

I laid down the book and opened my purse. "What time do you think we'll get into New York?" I asked.

The conductor looked at his watch before consulting the silver Hudson just visible through the speckled window. "We're making up time. Around eleven-forty maybe."

There would be time to knock off another few chapters before we arrived, and time to make the 12:45 screening. I'd already had a busy morning. Dr. Kleinz's medical experiments had followed a brief visit to the county coroner, a ponderous gentleman who was silent and skeptical with strangers. His written reports, though more forthcoming, had not been more suggestive. Henry Brook had consumed no more than one drink, and there were no indications of drugs. The injuries to his face were superficial scrapes and bruises, compatible with the idea that he had had a fall or been washed against the rocks of the jetty foundation. As to what had caused this fall or how the tideless lake had battered the body, the coroner had no ideas. He did not deal in theories, he told me, only facts. The body had spoken; Henry Brook had drowned.

Although I did not think much of the coroner's imaginative faculties, I had no reason to think him incompetent. If there was to be any clue to the motivations behind or circumstances around Brook's death, it lay outside the forensic evidence—perhaps even in the story or the script, for the further I got with both, the more I was struck by the oddity of the Kleinz role for a performer like Brook and the strangeness of the entire project for a director like Rossol. Despite the Holocaust details—and the Dachau chapter was certainly grim enough—*The Lazarus Gambit* was clearly more concerned with big bucks than big issues. I'd been assured that both actor and director were considered entirely "bankable," but with the current climate, a lot of bets were off. I wasn't the only one having trouble meeting my bills, and I couldn't help wondering if there hadn't been some fiscal trouble that had suddenly made this pop thriller attractive. It would be good to get Baby's report on Rossol's New Biograph Studio, and I decided to put her onto Brook's financial affairs as well. Until then, there was no point in theorizing. I began to skim the chapters that amplified the doctor's downhill slide from cooperation with the SS to human experimentation and morphine addiction. The scriptwriter, having less time, had simply moved from the scene of the subject's death to the final camp episode, a confrontation between Kleinz and the newly imprisoned Hanna. The scenario stipulated a freeze-frame shot of the doctor's doomed fiancée and then sent Kleinz off to a remote village high in the Alps, there to remain until late in the war when agents of the infamous Martin Bormann came knocking at the door of the doctor's chalet.

THE SCREENING ROOM was only a half dozen blocks from the station, ten floors up in an otherwise unremarkable building. There was a poky reception room plastered with a variety of notices and, behind a soundproof door, a smoky, shrunken movie theater where three perspiring gentlemen laden with film canisters were arguing at top volume. It was hard to determine where their grievances lay, because they were all shouting at once and gesturing with acrid cigarettes that added to the immediate impression of inadequate ventilation and cheap men's cologne. As I approached, one of them dashed his stack of film down on the nearest chair, and National Deluxe Screening Rooms appeared headed for a fistfight until the door of the projection booth banged open.

"What the hell's going on? Your hour is up. I've got other customers. Get that crap outta here."

There were gestures and exclamations from the trio down front, but since the projectionist was tall and lanky as well as nasty tempered, they eventually departed in a shower of obscene pleasantries and farewells, film canisters and scripts clutched in their arms.

"You next?" the projectionist bellowed. By voice, he was originally western, but he had adopted the pressured self-importance of the Big Apple; at some cost, it seemed, for when I walked to the back of the room, I noticed his teeth and fingers were stained yellow with nicotine.

"I'm Anna Peters from Independence Mutual to see *The Lazarus Gambit* film."

"They pay on time, at least," he said and jerked open the door of his booth. "It's all set for you. Rossol called this morning. You want 'em in any particular order?"

"Well—I think it would be easier if we could follow the plot line—at least as far as possible."

"Sure. Starting with?"

I took out my script. "What about this for today? The first meeting between Kleinz and Bormann, the bunker scenes, then the final Berlin scenes?"

"Okay. We've got reels from just before that, too." He reached over and ruffled the pages of the script. "This with Bormann and Morell was shot as well."

"What I'm chiefly interested in at the moment are Henry Brook's scenes."

"Oh, really?" The projectionist did a lot of work with his eyebrows, which is probably why they looked so thin and seedy. "Henry Brook fan, eh?"

"That's right."

"Hey, we get them all in here. That last crew was trying to decide how to improve a gay slasher flick. Improve! After you, we're booked to show three reels of *Strengthening Your Soybean Production*. You bring the film, we show it."

"*The Lazarus Gambit* should at least be entertaining."

"Box office gold, but I've seen enough of it," he said as he adjusted his projector. "Old Brookie took his time getting his act together. Any scene pales after the first fifty times."

"I didn't think unsatisfactory takes were printed."

"Most aren't but you gotta save some if there's usable stuff. Especially when you've got expensive effects going. And with Brookie you saved what you could get."

"I thought he was a very fine actor," I said, surprised.

"Sure he was. And a pain in the ass besides. We're all set. Go on down front."

"The footage that isn't any good—that has fluffs in it—what's done with that?" I asked quickly.

The projectionist shrugged. "Probably discard it. Maybe save some that can be cut into another take." He switched on the machine. "Take a seat, will you? I'm missing lunch to run this." He slammed the door of the booth and killed the lights so that I had to grope

my way to a seat, as a cell-like room with boarded-
over windows, a metal bed, and a few straight chairs
appeared on the screen. The camera made a quick pan
around a circle of hard-faced men in dark trenchcoats
and felt hats before coming to rest on Henry Brook,
who was sitting on a bare mattress, wearing hand-
cuffs. A fetlock of fair hair hung down into his eyes
and makeup had given him a nasty scrape on the left
side of his face that anticipated, in a most uncanny
way, the only visible injury to his corpse.

I found that disturbing, but otherwise the scene
with Kleinz, Bormann, and his henchmen was remarkable chiefly for the flashy camera angles and the
melodramatic, brownish lighting. It ended with the
doctor's agreeing to put a patient asleep in his esti-
vation process in return for an assortment of incrim-
inating documents and was followed by the now familiar repetitions and close-ups. I asked the
projectionist to skip these for the next sequence, set
in the bunkers under the Reich Chancellery where
Hitler and his court had huddled through the last days
of the war.

From the filmmaker's point of view, this episode
had represented logistical problems, for it was composed of several scenes shot in different locations.
First, Kleinz was shown arriving under guard in what
was really a rather beautiful scene with the smoking
rubble of Berlin photographed as delicately as morning fog. The footage took on a more appropriately
nightmarish quality when the party entered the un-
roofed, gargantuan hall of the Chancellery. Then the
camera shifted to the bottom of a passage in the bun-

ker to watch the Gestapo plainclothesmen, the SS guards, and Kleinz descend the narrow stairs.

The surprise of this segment was the revelation of the identity of Kleinz's patient, the heavily drugged Adolf Hitler, whose unfortunate double was already being cremated in the Chancellery gardens. Although there was plenty of dialogue and what appeared to be fairly complex bits of physical business, the take numbers were low. Clearly, Henry Brook had behaved himself better with Hitler than he had with the reichsführer.

The bunker scenes had been wrapped up efficiently, and once again, I marveled at the economical way Brook was able to convey emotion. When Bormann uncovered the patient's face and the camera swung down to reveal the dark features of Adolf Hitler, awe, hatred, fear—even a certain detached professional interest—were evident in Brook's gaunt face.

The whole sequence ended with what should have been Kleinz's execution, and Rossol had given the scene bravura treatment. It began with Kleinz and his SS escort silhouetted against the smoke and mist of the ruined gardens and ended with a sudden and spectacular explosion of bombs over the Chancellery. A great flash of orange light filled the screen, sending a shower of mud, rock, and debris over Kleinz and his would-be executioner. For a moment, new fires mingled with the black smoke floating through the garden, then the scene cleared to show a new bomb crater and, lying unconscious and mutilated beside it, the SS orderly, his pistol still in his outstretched hand. Kleinz, too, was sprawled motionless, but he gave a groan, opened his eyes, and raised his bleeding head.

"Terrific, huh?" the projectionist asked.

"Yeah, terrific, beautiful," I said, but I was wondering about the take numbers. They'd gone through the roof again. Brook had needed dozens of tries to manage what looked, at least to my untutored eyes, like a pretty straightforward tumble.

"Rossol may be a pain in the ass, but he sure can make movies," the projectionist said, threading up the last reel. "This is a terrific sequence. Helluva shame it's just to be left in the can."

"Yes," I said. "Is it complete?" I checked my script, but in the dim light the notations were confusing, and, not having the professional hardihood of the projectionist, I began to feel as if my eyes had been packed in salt.

"The Berlin stuff is. At last." His eyebrows made a complicated figure. "Pain and anguish in the making, what I hear."

"None of the outtakes are included in this batch, are they?"

"Oh, Christ, no! If you want to see those"—his eyebrows went frantic—"you'll have to come back. It's hours—hours."

"I'll think about it and call your secretary."

"Suit yourself. Who can afford, if not an insurance company?"

"What sort of sound for this?"

"You'll hear some. Rossol was going to add music and some highly distorted real sounds to suggest Kleinz's head injury." As he spoke, the projectionist cut the lights, and Kleinz ran across the screen into the swirling mist and smoke of the garden. "Heartbeat here, I think. Luba, duba, big drumming sound."

"Nice."

"Yeah, and watch this," he exclaimed with genuine pleasure as Kleinz ran past the whitened carcasses
of shops and apartments. Between the buildings the
paving was opened by vast water-filled shell craters,
but even in this horrific scene, Rossol's aesthetic
sense had dominated. The figures were beautifully
composed against the dust and clouds, the grayed-out
colors as elegant as old tintypes, and when Kleinz
plunged into a subway tunnel to elude some Russian
troops, the underground became a startling sequence
of bold lights and shadows.

"Like *Caligari*," I suggested.

"Oh, yes," said the projectionist, pleased. "He
hates realism. You wouldn't want this looking like a
forties battle picture. And look at this—done with
models." He pointed through the glass window of the
booth toward a sharply angled shot of the Brandenburg Gate with a red flag already hanging from one
side.

"Love it, don't you? Hitchcock couldn't have done
that better."

"Right. Where are we now?"

"Our hero's escape from Berlin," the projectionist
said. The clips ended with the shore of a lake, the
corpses of Hitler Youth, and the doctor's departure
via rowboat across the Havel. The camera pulled very
far back to show him, tiny and alone, drifting on a
dull silver sheet of water.

"Ahhh," said the projectionist with satisfaction.
"Beautiful and so German."

"German?"

"Like *Lohengrin*, where the hero drifts off in the swan boat."

"This one isn't much of a hero."

"I was speaking technically." His skillful fingers slid across the dials of the projector. "That's it for today. You want the Latin American scenes next time?"

"How many is Brook in?"

"Not a lot."

"I'll see those." I thought a moment, then took out a hundred-dollar bill. "For yourself. Find me the out-takes from Brook's work for the Berlin scenes."

"For another of these, I might turn something up."

"Cash on delivery," I said as I left the booth. "I'll phone when I'm ready to see the footage."

"Send in the next crew," he called after me. "I'm ready for the soybeans."

In the lobby downstairs, I tried unsuccessfully to call Brook's wife and girlfriend but had better luck with his costar for the Latin American segment. Altheia Karl was at home and could see me around seven. I retrieved my case from Grand Central, checked into the exorbitant digs secured by the largesse of Independence Mutual, then walked up along the twilight park and across to Madison, where the actress had an apartment on the seventh floor of an elegant old building. I was greeted by a woman speaking an unrecognizable language, who motioned me into a huge open-plan apartment with pale walls, soft leather furniture, and very beautiful patterned rugs and tapestries. She gestured for me to sit down in the living room.

"Maria!" a husky voice called. "This damn dress! I need help!"

The woman smiled apologetically and covered the fifty feet or so to the back of the apartment at top speed. Meanwhile, I took in the well-planted balcony off the living room, the high ceilings, and matched rosewood, and thought that such opulence was a good recommendation for a career in the movies. After a few minutes, the slap of bare feet on the parquetry announced the actress, who came striding into the room, wearing a magnificent, heavy white silk evening dress and carrying a pair of gold slippers.

"Anna Peters? Altheia Karl. Sit down. Forgive the chaos. I'm tearing off to a party for a producer."

She spoke in a breathless rush, swishing her glorious blond mane back and forth across her shoulders before plumping down onto one of the couches. She curled her long legs beneath her and dropped the shoes with a clatter. "What would you like to drink?"

"I'm fine, thanks," I said.

"That's right. You're working. Insurance. What a bore. But I don't mean to be rude," she added quickly.

"Not at all. Normally, it is very boring."

Her housekeeper appeared.

"Some tomato juice, please, Maria. Not even some juice, Ms. Peters?"

"A small glass of tomato juice, thanks."

"I never drink, either," she said. "Except champagne. I think champagne is very good for you."

I nodded. Whatever she drank, the rest of us should try. Altheia Karl was the most glamorous creature I'd ever seen. She was beautiful for starters, tall and luxuriously constructed, with fine, regular features. New York is full of pretty women, and beauty is almost *de rigueur* for a movie star. What made her different was the impression of absolute flawlessness. There was not a mark, a wrinkle, a freckle, or a scar on her skin, and she was showing off a good deal of it in her remarkably engineered gown. She was perfectly proportioned and extremely graceful, with the unselfconsciousness of a large, fair cat. Indeed, except for the touch of daring in her plunging neckline and the immense butterfly pendant that ornamented it, she might have suffered the fate of Byron's heroine who endured the worst of faults, perfection.

"Cheers," she said.

"Cheers."

"You said something about the insurance?"

"Just routine. As you can imagine, Ms. Karl, there was a lot of money tied up in the insurance package for *The Lazarus Gambit* and also for Henry Brook's personal coverage."

"Dear, you don't have to mention it. I'm told my own premiums are astronomical." She smiled with unaffected pleasure. "Though, of course, I'm more reliable and healthy as a horse."

"What about Henry Brook?"

"Well, he was starting to look his age." She was thoughtful for a moment. "I don't think he was awfully well, but there were reasons."

I tried to conceal my interest. "What were they?"

"He lived a very unhealthy life," she said severely. "I realize other people think performers narcissistic, but we have to take care of our instrument. I don't smoke; I don't drink; I exercise daily. I take dance class, it's so much better for you than jogging. Swimming, dance, horseback riding—stick with those.''

''I'm inclined to take your advice.''

''I'm sort of a nut for fitness,'' she admitted, ''but Henry had no sense.''

I waited.

''He was just always running around. A real satyr.''

''Perhaps he didn't care for dance or swimming.''

''Now you're being naughty. I'm not sure that's sound in an insurance agent,'' she said. I realized I'd have to be careful; she was quicker than she let on at first.

''I'm an insurance investigator. A certain irreverence is considered desirable.''

I got the wide, beautiful smile.

''So who was Brook chasing?'' I asked.

''Who could he catch? He really wasn't the sort of man you enjoy going to bed with when the cameras are running.'' She made a face. ''Thank heaven there was always a crowd. But it was difficult, although I'm getting much better at the bedroom stuff. I do a very fine orgasm.'' She tipped her head back and fluttered her eyes before she broke into a laugh. ''Off camera,'' she added primly, ''I stayed away from him.''

''Presumably others were less prudent?''

''Oh, yes. Let's see. His wife was there. His ex-wife. I think that's tacky, don't you? I think you should be divorced or not. I hate these halfway arrangements.''

''How did they get on?''

''Fine. He insulted her and she bullied him.''

''About what? The bullying, I mean.''

"His life. It was fortunate she was along, or he'd never have made a call. And Belinda, of course—"

"Belinda is—?"

"Designated girlfriend. A sniveling thing. I don't think she weighs a hundred pounds," Altheia said, shifting her own nicely distributed weight in one rippling motion. "They used her as the girl in the concentration camp scene. I mean, she was realistic."

"Not quite the type one would imagine."

"Any type for him."

"And what about Len Rossol?" I asked. "I suspect he has inclinations along those lines too."

"Oh, he's quite different," she said and grinned. "Many an actress owes her start to his appetite."

"So the two of them got on? Boys together on the prowl?"

"Neither is a pack animal. I've the idea feelings got a tiny bit out of control."

"Over what? Or should I say whom?"

"Belinda, of all people."

"I don't imagine that helped the production," I said though some other angles came to mind.

"I don't know," Altheia said. "I'm not at all sure."

"I thought there were problems keeping everything on schedule."

"Oh, yes, it was a disaster from a fiscal point of view. Money wasted; time wasted. I've barely two weeks vacation before I fly off to Rome."

I remembered to be polite and inquired about this new role.

"A sister in a cloistered order," she said, "who's burning for a handsome young nobleman."

"Sounds challenging."

She laughed. "You're not serious."

"But *The Lazarus Gambit*...you were saying—"

"Yes, I was just going to say that in spite of all the aggro there was an electric atmosphere on the set. Brook could be remarkable."

"A tremendous privilege to work with?"

Again the shake of the golden mane and the big and, now I realized, slightly wicked smile. "You've been talking to Lani Dupres." She clutched her throat and drew in her shoulders. "'To work with the great man in his last role.' She has perverted tastes, don't you think?"

I evaded this question as tactfully as possible.

"Still, it was extraordinary. We were all so good. I'm not usually hired for my acting genius, you know," she said good-naturedly. "But I did some remarkable scenes. It's possible it was all Len's idea of a psychodrama to get us into the parts. He wanted"—she stopped and considered—"he wanted to take a cheap, melodramatic story and get the energy out of the violence, the sex, you know, and use it artistically. I'd have said that would work, but..." She shrugged.

"I saw the Berlin sequence today. It was very handsome."

"He wanted to get people caught up in the story. He had this theory that there's too big a separation between pop stuff and art. Pop's got plot and action, art's got characters and style. He wanted to put both together."

"For a smash hit."

"Yes, he wanted that too," she admitted. "And I thought Brook wanted that as well."

"But he wasn't holding up his end?"

"Well, only after dozens of takes. He was late, Ms. Peters. He was unreliable. He fought with Rossol, and he and his ex-wife..." She rolled her greenish eyes. "Not to mention the carryings-on with Belinda."

Something in her look made me wonder if her extraordinary glamour did not exclude desire on her own part. Her perfection might stem from an unusually self-contained and self-sufficient personality.

"You also said he might not have been too well," I prompted.

"He complained a couple of times. The Berlin sequence I'm told was a nightmare. Complaints of one sort or another. Ours—the ones we shot—were quite smooth."

I opened my case for the script. "You'd done some interior scenes with Brook?"

"That's right. We used a house upstate. Of course, we were all going to Argentina for the outdoor scenes in the city. And we'd have done the big party scene here in the studio. It was set for this week." She gave a sad smile.

"The party scene?" I ruffled the pages, but she explained.

"Big audience-recognition scene. I was to wear this." She touched the pendant. "Kleinz's ever-so-convenient girlfriend, his solace in exile, is also an Israeli secret agent, code name Butterfly."

"That seems almost excessive."

"No, no, it was fun. I put my hair up and looked very severe and dedicated. I loved that. I think I'll make a good nun after all. Which would surprise a lot of people. Anyway, the audience doesn't know about my secret life and neither does Kleinz. They just know that the Israeli agents are lurking about to meet Butterfly. I go to a party, but I'm shown in an evening cloak or in tight close-up until the script calls for the camera to move up on the agents watching the group from a balcony above the dance floor. They look over the crowd and the camera zooms in on my pendant.''

"Very Hitchcockian."

"Just what Len said! A little homage to the master."

"I'm sure it would have been very effective."

"Yes. Well, Ms. Peters, is that it?"

"Just one last thing. What would you say Brook's attitude was? Was he happy, depressed? What would you say?"

"Oh, the classic question. Well, he wasn't a happy man. Not at all, but I'm not sure he was ever any different. I don't think he was depressed at all. He was—I don't know whether I'd say he was very emotional or very unemotional, now that I think of it. He needed a lot of emotional scenes. Big fights, artistic crises, dramas. Does that necessarily mean he was emotional?"

Interesting. She was the second person to make that observation. "But he didn't seem upset about any one thing?"

She shook her head and I stood up.

"Thank you. You've been very helpful. I hope your trip to the convent is a great success."

"Be sure to see it. *Rose of Lombardy.* Can you

believe that title?'' She laughed and called for her housekeeper to let me out. I walked back to the hotel in a thoughtful mood: I had spent two full days listening to information about Henry Brook, and his colleagues seemed to be remembering him with less and less affection as the shock of his death receded. That was depressing. He had been so charming, so funny, so moving on the screen; now those memories were eroded by the knowledge that he'd been predatory, unprofessional, self-centered, and emotionally exhibitionistic.

"Don't ever learn about movie stars," I told Harry that night on the phone.

"So don't tell me anything," he said. "It's your business to be disillusioned."

"Oh, thanks. What are you doing? I can hear mazurkas." That meant Jan Gorgon, his business partner, was in the studio.

"Jan says it's his saint's day or something."

"More likely he's made a big sale."

"That too, I think. He was asking about your rent check. I said you'd sent it."

"Wish I had." I rent space for Executive Security in the partnership's building, the rest of which is devoted to Harry's graphics workshop and Jan's antique and art importing business. "Next week. Tell him I'm getting a big fee from Independence Mutual."

"You're not really having difficulties?"

"No, no," I said too quickly. Jan handles the money; Harry takes care of the artistic side and adds an air of integrity.

"Because maybe we can make some arrangement."

"I don't want to get you involved."

"Listen, you've helped support the workshop."

"We'll talk about it. But if I can get regular work from Independence Mutual...."

"Oh, I almost forgot. Baby came in with a message for you. She said you were expecting it."

I sat up on the bed and reached for my notebook. "What did she find?"

"Let's see: 'Rossol's studio, despite the success of *Angel Street* and the coproduction of *Star Wizard,* is rumored to be in serious financial trouble.'"

"Did she say why?"

"'Cost of setting up studio facilities in New York, expensive technical equipment, problems with the budget of his last picture.'"

"That would have been *Borodino.*"

"It did well but didn't have legs, the overseas and television sales haven't been up to expectations. The main problem, though, seems to have been the cost of the studio. She's got a note that the motivation for the move east seems pretty much just to have been his distaste for Hollywood."

"What about his assets?"

"He has some. He produced *Gang of Four,* which has done well, and the compilation, *Hollywood Funnymen.* Those have kept him afloat, but evidently, he needed *The Lazarus Gambit* badly."

"And now he needs the insurance money, and fairly quickly, too."

"That would bail him out according to what Baby says here."

"I guess I'd better get on with the investigation. I'd hate to be the cause of his financial collapse."

"It's not up to you, though, is it?"

"Not really. From what I hear, the company is quite satisfied that the picture can't be completed. A good third of Brook's scenes hadn't been shot when he died. If he hadn't been such a prima donna, they'd have had the bulk of the stuff in the can."

"I wonder if Rossol could have finished the picture anyway," Harry said thoughtfully.

"What do you mean?"

"Well, Baby has something here about financing difficulties and notes due. Perhaps you'd better call her at home. It's just a quick note she'd typed and it's pretty sketchy."

"Perhaps I'd better. Thanks a lot, dear."

"It's okay. When do you think you'll be home?"

"I'm not sure. I've got people to see, some more film to run, a couple of days probably. I'll call you tomorrow."

We said goodbye, and I hung up feeling lonely and a bit guilty. To tell the truth, I was two months behind in the rent and that got on my nerves. The last few years, I'd gotten used to prosperity; a good cash flow had enabled me to ignore the fact that Executive Security was still undercapitalized. And Len Rossol was in the same boat! I suppressed a twinge of sympathy and spent the rest of the evening trying to connect with Baby, whose social life, although considerably reduced from a few years ago, was still remarkably lively. In between, I read up on Dr. Kleinz's reemergence as a respectable doctor named Rund whose wartime misdeeds had been conveniently erased by his head injury in the Chancellery gardens. His taste for research survived, however, for he took an opportunity to study tropical fevers in Latin America. There he met Altheia impersonating a German-Swiss social worker, aka Agent Butterfly, and began a romance in the best tradition of big-scale thrillers. Their first dramatic tryst was interrupted by the telephone. It was Baby at last, and as she filled in the details of Rossol's precarious finances, I began to understand his distaste for Ed Martins and his anxiety to speed up the insurance procedure. At the time of Brook's death, he'd been only a couple of weeks from fiscal catastrophe.

SIX

Marylin and Henry Brook had lived in an attractive part of Greenwich Village, amid tree-lined streets of mellowed brick and stone houses. I arrived there early, the nicest time in New York, when the gasoline-tinged air was still clear, and the low, bright sun caught the tops of the hedges, lingered on the soft buff and sienna walls, and brightened the coats of the passersby and the first tulips in the little park. Except for the pervasive earthy and acrid smells left by the city's dogs—now confined for the day, poor urban beasts—everything was charming. I was in a cheerful mood as I passed a privet hedge guarded by spiked ironwork and rang the bell. I had a minute to admire the neighbor's window boxes and hear the pizzicato of fashionable shoes and an exchange of taxi horns before the door opened.

"I'm Anna Peters," I said, "from Independence Mutual."

"It's about time."

"Are you Mrs. Brook?" I asked, but there was no doubt. She was a woman of maybe forty-five, tanned enough to look artificial among the pale northerners. Less well preserved than her husband, she had some gray in her dark, tangled hair, and, despite the rose-tinted glasses, I could see puffy tracks around her hard, protruding blue eyes. Although her coiffure was still unfinished, she was otherwise fully rigged out in a peculiarly bohemian business suit of maroon tweed, fringed at every possible edge. This was worn with an expensive silk plaid blouse in matching murky colors, dark, patterned stockings, and maroon boots. The impression of well-heeled eccentricity was completed by a mass of Indian silver jewelry, African beads, and old-fashioned diamond rings. It took me a moment to absorb all this, but Mrs. Brook was already launched.

"I expected you people to have had everything settled already," she complained. "It's been two weeks. Come in, I don't want to discuss business out on the stoop. I've been calling and calling. The head office has been informed."

"I've been asked to make a few inquiries," I said.

"You'd better have come to discuss the policy." She closed the door with a bang.

The foyer was a departure from the clean eighteenth-century facade outside, being crammed with Victorian furniture, theatrical posters, and mementos. These, though handsome, were marred by the slovenly clutter: papers, soiled clothes, cosmetics, handbags, and a vast assortment of hairpins. Mrs. Brook picked up a handful of these and began to straighten her disheveled locks. "I can't believe the treatment I've had from your company. It's been most inconsiderate. Henry wasn't an ordinary man, you realize. I imagine even insurance agents have heard of Henry Brook."

I murmured that he had been a great actor. I was adding my sympathy when she broke in. "An actor of genius. It's obvious even to the"—she looked at me as if searching for the proper designation—"uninitiated. He was a wonder, a genius, but so impractical. I handled everything, even after the divorce. I know you will think that extraordinary! Not many women would bother to keep their ex-husband afloat. But he was like a child. No thought for money. Despite everything I could do, Henry's financial affairs had a way of..." She gave a sour smile and began turning the diamond rings on her fingers around and around.

"I think I understand."

"I doubt it," she said briskly. "No one knows what it's like to live with such a talent. Or with a man who is so...generous." She looked a little frantic. "That's why I must insist on action on Henry's policy. His affairs are in a mess as usual and who's left to straighten them out?"

I heard her loud and clear: the money was needed.

"We'll do everything we can, but you understand that with so large a policy it is routine to ask a few questions."

"I know how the business is supposed to operate," she said belligerently. "My lawyers—"

"Please, Mrs. Brook. I have no control over payment of benefits. If I can just make my report, everything will go smoothly." I hoped so, anyway; I was rather exceeding my commission in troubling the grieving widow.

She gave me a glassy stare, then walked into the living room, which, like the entranceway, was an admirable but untidy room. Nothing in it seemed exactly clean, and there was a fusty, closed-up smell overlaid with a whiff of alcohol.

"Well," she demanded. We were still standing.

I took out my notebook, sat on the edge of a chair,

and tried to look official. "Your husband had been in good health?"

"The doctors examined him before the picture started. Before the policy was granted."

"I just wondered, because as I understand it, there had been a number of delays in the shooting. Because of his complaints of illness."

"Nothing serious. Henry was high-strung."

"Strung out, more likely," said a clear, high voice. A very self-possessed child was standing in the doorway. Or rather, she looked like a child, but a second glance corrected this impression. Slight and small-boned but tall and very leggy, she was dressed in a pseudo convent-school costume of black skirt and bolero jacket, expensive organdy sailor blouse, fine black stockings, and flat shoes. The skirt was about a foot shorter than any reputable order would have countenanced, and she was wearing deep purple-red lipstick, lots of eye shadow, and a very sophisticated perfume. Despite these accoutrements, she was not unappealing. And probably no more than sixteen or seventeen.

"I'm Belinda Tayana. Are you from the insurance company?"

Mrs. Brook made a considerable business out of checking her watch. "Belinda, dear, this is money."

"That's why I'm here, of course. Marylin's afraid our Henry might have left me more than was proper."

"You have an appointment in half an hour," Mrs. Brook reminded her. "See you're not late."

"I'm already made up and dressed." With childish pleasure, she pivoted for Mrs. Brook's inspection.

"Your collar's not straight." She fixed this, looked

the girl over, then nodded. "A child molester's dream."

Belinda had a high, silvery laugh. "Don't tell her any lies about me. You won't, will you?"

Marylin Brook's face was hard and expressionless. "Don't be such a little bitch, Belinda."

"We're shooting down on Washington Square," the girl said, looking at me. "Stop by. If you buy me an expensive lunch, I'll tell you lots of things." She stepped away quickly and grabbed her purse from a table near the door.

Mrs. Brook flushed but controlled herself. "You're not talented enough to make scenes, dear."

The silvery laugh came from the hall before the door opened and closed. When Belinda was gone, Marylin's expression turned tragic. "In his later years, Henry could be so difficult. No one who hasn't taken care of a genius can imagine."

"She's a model?" I glanced toward the door

"One of the hottest at the moment. She makes absolutely obscene wages."

I wondered if that was why she was still allowed to hang about the Brook residence but didn't ask.

"Henry discovered her, of course. He had an eye for talent. He could have made his living as an agent." She twisted her mouth. "I must ask you to ignore the gossip, the malicious gossip. And Belinda's fantasies. You can do that." It was not a question.

"I'm not interested in gossip, Mrs. Brook."

"Call me Marylin." It was not a request. She had a way of making simple courtesies somehow offensive.

"All right, Marylin. I realize this is difficult, but it is all routine. As you know, the coroner has already found your husband's death to be misadventure."

"Yes," she said coldly, "so there are really no more questions."

Apparently she had saved the big scenes for Henry; she seemed very much in control at the moment.

"Not officially. Unofficially, I think you'll admit it was a freakish accident."

"A drowning at night? Unfortunately, that's not so unusual."

"It's unusual to be in the water in New York State in April. And the lake is shallow near the shore. No more than three, four feet." I wondered if she'd know that. Maybe not.

"There was a party." The lines on her face deepened into a tragic mask and tears came into her eyes. For some reason I remembered Lani Dupres's ability to weep on cue.

"He hadn't had anything much to drink had he?"

She shook her head, sighed, and raised her diamond-encrusted hands. Perhaps she had real sorrow but could only express it in this theatrical manner. I took this moment to ask what I really wanted to know. "He couldn't swim, I suppose?"

"Swim? Bates Swim Team. One of his great vanities."

"So I don't understand—" I began.

"A fall. They think he took a fall."

"Yes, that's probably right. But I wonder how and why he fell. How he fell hard enough, when he was sober, to remain unconscious when he hit that cold water. Why he didn't just stand up and climb out. It's rather bothered me.''

There was a silence. Maybe it had bothered her too.

''Was there some trouble on the set?'' I asked cautiously.

''What sort of trouble?''

''The picture was behind schedule. I know that, because Independence Mutual carried the policy on *The Lazarus Gambit* as well as on your husband. Had things been going smoothly, most of the picture would have been completed.''

''Henry was a perfectionist. A great artist,'' she said quickly. ''He wanted everything to be just right. Some people don't care about perfection. What's good enough will do.''

''Which category is Leonard Rossol in?''

''He's overrated. Very much overrated.''

''Was there any friction between them?'' But this was going too far, and she was immediately on her guard. I recognized the formal, speaking-for-the-record tone that I'd heard from other cast members.

''Henry was always professional. Less talented performers…there's malice, insecurity. But that's nothing to do with your business.'' She gave me a hard look and stood up.

''And Henry's health?''

''You have the medical report. Look it up.'' She turned her wrist to see her watch. ''I've an appointment. And I must look in on Belinda. She quite depends on me.''

I couldn't help wondering in what way.

''I must say I'm not pleased about your visit,'' she said as we walked to the door. ''I had expected action on the policy instead of a lot of questions. I believe I'll complain to the company—to the home office."

"That's your privilege."

I got a sour look and the door slammed. Marylin Brook was used to pulling rank—an occupational hazard, no doubt, for wives and managers of successful actors. Since that was only one of the unpleasant things suggested by the Brook residence, I decided Valon and Independence Mutual would have to absorb the cost of an expensive lunch, and set out for Washington Square Park.

Belinda was near the arch, along with two other models similarly togged out, an older woman in a nun's habit with an immense old-fashioned white wimple, and a lean and noisy photographer accompanied by his assistants. To my untrained eyes, they seemed to be making heavy weather of a picture of three pretty girls on a nice day, but no doubt that's how Belinda's "obscene" wages were justified. Everything was set up again and again. The "nun" was directed diagonally across the opening of the arch, followed by the three models, who were supposedly her charges. The key thing seemed to be the breeze, which was supposed to ruffle their skirts and make them clutch their white straw hats. To the amusement of the spectators, the wind either refused to come or came so violently that it disarranged the models' hair, necessitating the ministrations of an excitable lady whose apparently unlimited supply of hairspray was concealed under a voluminous cape. Finally, however, the picture was pronounced a success. It was the last of the day. The models put on their topcoats, returned the neat little purses they'd carried to the hairdresser, and checked their watches. Belinda alone seemed to have no other appointments.

"You came," she said.

"I was invited."

She looked over her shoulder and gave a little wave to her colleagues. "Somewhere extravagant."

"Somewhere expensive," I corrected.

After some negotiation, we settled on a French restaurant that suited her without entirely bankrupting me, and I stepped to the curb to hail a cab.

"Hurry up," she said. "Marylin will be here."

"Does she always pick you up?"

"Often. She should be here," she added anxiously. "She's almost always on time."

"Would you rather wait for her?"

"No, no, I don't want to see her," she said, but she dithered back and forth as if anxious for Mrs. Brook to appear. Once a cab arrived, though, every trace of nervousness vanished. She was like a kid on a treat, and when we arrived at the restaurant and were shown to what she pronounced "a good table," she seemed positively delighted. Then she assumed an air of innocent excitement, which, I suspected, was calculated to make me look predatory, and began whispering flirtatiously. Belinda Tayana was a complicated young woman.

"Don't strain yourself," I said. "This is strictly business."

She was not at all put out. I suppose in her own way she was quite amusing. Perhaps that's what Brook had liked about her.

"You're some sort of detective, aren't you?"

"I suppose you could stretch 'insurance investigator' that far."

"I'm glad you've come. Can I have champagne?"

"If you don't have too much."

"I've met someone who says it's very healthy."

"So have I."

Our eyes met for an instant, and I could see she was surprised and a little uneasy. When she spoke, she was serious. "I am glad you've come. I was sorry about Henry. Really sorry." I sensed regret but not real grief.

"He gave you a start?"

"Yes. He bought me, more or less, from Mommy."

"What's the more or less mean?"

"He got her to let me come live with them. To get into modeling."

"That's the less. What's the more?"

She wrinkled up her nose. "He gave her a check, and she didn't try to make a scandal."

"Was there a scandal to make?"

"Not a very big scandal. I was fifteen."

"Just the right-sized scandal."

"You could say that. I thought it was kind of silly, but it worked okay. We needed the money."

"And now, I'm told, you're making it hand over fist and living rent free."

"Rent free, but I buy the food. Until Henry's... things are settled."

There was a pause. Waiters came, stealthy as assassins, to present little nests of pink shrimp, and I considered the implications of Belinda's life at the Brook's. Could Mrs. Brook really need the girl's wages? That was interesting and so was Belinda. I had to admit she was not the Sunset Strip cutie with dyed hair and vulgar clothes that I'd expected. Belinda had swanky manners and perfect grammar. She was, if anything, rather formal. I imagined good schools, travel, comfort—then a reversal in fortune that forced her mother to live by her wits. I suspected that was how Belinda was going to manage too and felt a sudden kinship. Uneducated young women need a lot of wit and a lot of luck if they're not to wind up in trouble. I'd had a bit of both, plus the inestimable good fortune of meeting Harry before I got too far out of line. Belinda had met Henry Brook and Len Rossol—more famous but not, I thought, so nice.

"Were you fond of Henry?"

Belinda bit her lip and looked, for the first time, like a teenage girl. "Yes."

"But not in love with him?"

She shook her head.

"What about Leonard Rossol? There's a dynamic man."

A little shadow crossed her face, and I decided she was piquant rather than pretty. "Henry'd promised me a part in the movies," she said, as if this explained volumes.

"Well, he managed that. Didn't you die pathetically in Dr. Kleinz's experiment?"

"But I had no lines." She didn't sound spoiled, just hardheaded. Henry Brook had been foolish if he'd made any exaggerated commitments to her.

"Len Rossol, now—"

"There might be a part," she said in a tiny, childish voice. She picked daintily at the shrimp. "I don't think Henry should have been angry—I mean, I can't be held totally to his deal with Mommy, can I?''

"That seems to me a scandalous question."

She giggled. "That's what I said. He didn't always have a sense of humor."

"Men don't have as much humor as they like to think."

"No." The champagne bubbled in the thin tulip-shaped glasses. She took a sip. "Not bad. You don't live like this all the time, do you?"

"Nor you, either. You'd get too fat."

"For modeling." But her smile was wistful. "I'm going to get a little money. From Henry."

"A little?"

"There might have been more than that, but..." She shrugged. "I really didn't care about the money. I cared for my part and the people I met and the modeling fees, but I didn't care about Henry's money."

I was inclined to believe her. She was intelligent, perhaps intelligent enough not to sacrifice long-term opportunities for short-term gains.

"Would you kill someone over something like that, over leaving money to the wrong person?" She had a way of asking the right question at the surprising time.

"It's been done," I said.

"I got hysterical when they found Henry. I was so afraid."

"Why were you afraid?"

"How did he die?" She leaned back and watched as the waiter slid away the appetizers and produced the soup.

"The coroner says by 'misadventure.' He fell, scraped his face, rolled into the water, and drowned."

"You don't die that way."

"You can, but it needs an explanation. Determination, a head injury. Something."

"I didn't think he was that upset. I didn't mean for him to be that upset."

I took out a tissue, and she wiped her eyes, removing a swath of her violet shadow.

"There were a lot of fights," she said. "I just thought—what's one more, you know."

"Maybe that was true. Maybe he wasn't that upset."

"I didn't think he was. And if he wasn't, I don't want Marylin to get the money. I'll say he was upset. I'll say it was all because of me."

"Marylin says you tell lies," I remarked.

"Sometimes I do."

"Why don't you want her to have the money? She seems to have worked hard to keep her husband financially stable."

"Her ex-husband."

"Her ex-husband financially stable," I corrected myself. "So why shouldn't she have the money?"

Belinda looked up, frightened, sophisticated, sly. "Because I think she murdered him."

SEVEN

"Why do you think Mrs. Brook murdered her husband?" I asked.

"Because of me, of course. It didn't work out the way she'd thought. 'One of Henry's little interests, one of Henry's little things.' I'm never going to be a little anything," Belinda said.

"My impression is that you didn't take Henry Brook all that seriously. A smart woman like Marylin Brook could have waited things out."

"Uh-uh. It was Henry." She set her elbows on the table and leaned forward. "He just wasn't reasonable. He thought I would marry him, you know. He said he wanted to start over fresh."

I considered this. Henry Brook had been just about the right age for such foolishness. And if he were divorced... "He could have married you? He and Marylin really were—"

"Oh, yes. Divorced three years ago. But he was too good a business for her to drop out of the picture, and he couldn't do without her. Well, he couldn't till I came along. I'm pretty good about money."

"I see." The comfortable and profitable ménage had threatened to form a new configuration. "How come you've stayed with her?"

"Well, I didn't know anyone else, and she does know an awful lot. And then there's the insurance money, though I shouldn't discuss that with you."

"No, that's very prudent. How much has she promised you?"

"She's going to help me get to the European collection showings. And some, a little, to get me started. An apartment..." She shrugged eloquently.

"Very generous, considering."

"That's when I knew."

I raised my eyebrows.

"Knew she killed him."

"Not good enough."

"You think I'm making it up," she said, pouting. "You don't believe me."

"Not enough information. Motive? Maybe. But opportunity, means?"

"We were all at the party."

"All right, that's opportunity. But the fact that you were all at the party and that no one seems sure when people left weakens your case. Then there's the means."

"I'm afraid anyway," said Belinda.

I took a sip of champagne, then another, the bubbles tingling my nose. Strictly speaking, Belinda was not my worry. "Have you a friend?" I asked. "Another model? A young woman you could plausibly bring home to stay with you?"

"There are a few. No one I really, really like."

"Don't be too fussy. Call one of your friends. Think up a story and get her to move in with you and Marylin."

"What will I tell Marylin?"

"That's your department. Think of something that's not too melodramatic. Have you a lawyer?"

She nodded, her face suddenly serious. One part of

her was worldly and malicious; the other part was young, ordinary, and scared.

"Explain your situation. Find out where you stand financially. You may be able to turn down Mrs. Brook's kind offer."

"I want a big dessert," Belinda said.

I signaled the waiter. She ordered a fudge sundae with all the trimmings, and I ordered melon.

"Marylin doesn't allow me," she explained. "Not good for my weight."

"But you're hoping to go to Hollywood, where you won't have to stay emaciated."

"I'm not sure I'll get there now."

"No? You wouldn't have married Henry Brook, anyway, would you?"

"Oh, no, not Henry. I was pretty much through with him, to tell you the truth. I'll be eighteen in December. I won't be a minor anymore. I can live where I want. I thought—well, it was pretty certain I was going to join Leonard Rossol when he went back to the Coast."

I had a little more of the good champagne and remembered Gloria and the faint, sly smile Lani Dupres had worn sitting beside the director at dinner. This child had been willing to take on a lot.

"That's why there was trouble between him and Henry," she continued. "At first it was fun. You know, a big rivalry."

I knew, and I also knew Belinda was too young to see that passionate rivalries have a way of becoming consuming, but strictly masculine, affairs. With those star egos, she'd have vanished in the fracas. "Pistols at dawn are out of style," I observed.

"They did other things." She toyed with her immense mound of chocolate sauce and whipped cream.

"Such as?"

"Extra shots, being late on the set, flubbing lines. And on Len's side, making utterly unreasonable demands. I think Henry got the best of it. He could goof a line a dozen different ways but do it perfectly just like that, the minute before he'd have gone too far."

"That picture cost in excess of forty million dollars, Belinda. The profits from it were apparently as important to Henry as they were to Rossol, who was producing as well as directing. Although you're attractive—"

"You don't think they liked me that much."

"Let's say I find it hard to believe they'd put sentiment ahead of profits."

"It got started," she said softly. "It just got started. One day everything was fine. You know, I'd flirt with Rossol and that made it better with Henry." She broke off and glanced about the restaurant, finding support in the elegant diners, the soft, expensive decor, white linens, and silent dessert trolleys. Everything around us said money and hinted success. "It was just playing. I mean there'd been no big romance with Henry whatever he thought. And Marylin was always around." She took an enormous stab out of the sundae as if in defiance of the adult world. It seemed to me that she knew too much about one facet of life and next to nothing about the rest.

"Then, you know, something happened. Nothing was fun anymore. Everyone was nervous and sour."

"And the picture?"

"Delayed. But everyone said it was good…if they could just get it finished."

I began to wonder if abandoning the film had been a real possibility. If so, Brook's death had been a lucky accident for the filmmakers, a bad break for Independence Mutual.

"And so things are off with Rossol?"

"Nothing is fun anymore," she said firmly. She pushed back her sundae. "I've got to go. We're fitting for a big show later this afternoon."

"All right." I waved to the waiter. "You can get in touch if you have problems."

"What sort of problems?" she asked, deliberately obtuse.

"You said you were frightened."

"I don't know what you can do about that."

"Probably nothing." Nonetheless, I mentioned my hotel and she wrote down my room number.

"Will you drop me off?" she asked.

"Sure." I could see that she liked to have things done for her—little favors, treats—and wondered if that was Marylin's hold over her; nothing sinister, just a precocious kid's need for someone to lean on. And Marylin was formidable enough not to make dependence seem too obvious. If I was right, that was the last detail in a picture that was plausible, if not neat, and when I returned to the hotel for my messages, I considered calling Valon and making my report. From Independence Mutual's perspective, it wasn't a good one: Brook had been a good swimmer, which ruled out panic in the water. He had had personal problems and professional difficulties, and although I should wait for Baby's report, I smelled money troubles. All

these hinted at suicide, but there wasn't a shred of
hard evidence, and it didn't look as if there was going
to be any. As for Belinda's accusations, they were
probably only nerves and imagination. Brook had aggravated a number of people, including Belinda, Rossol, and a substantial portion of the cast and crew, as
well as his ex-wife, but he was too important eco-
nomically for any one of them to bump him off. The
verdict was "not proven," as the Scots say, and Independence Mutual would have to settle.

"Ms. Peters?" The desk clerk had returned to the
counter with another slip of paper.

"Yes."

"Another message. It had fallen down. I'm sorry."

"No problem." It was from McNab, the estate
caretaker, who informed me that the younger Mr. Delf
had decided to open the house early after all. He was
expected midafternoon.

Damn. The clock above the counter said ten past
three. If it had been even five, I could have found
some excuse, but as it was, I had plenty of time to
drive upstate. I was strongly tempted to ignore the
note, call Valon, and get back to Harry, D.C., and my
outstanding bills, but instead I returned to the desk
and called for a car.

One of the fallacies of urban life is that efficiency
rises with concentration of services. In the abstract,
maybe; in New York, the point of diminished returns
has long been passed. Although the nearest rental garage was a mere five blocks away, it was a full hour
before I was ensconced in a Datsun whose sporty
lines and elegant slanted glass ensured a good sunny-
day grilling. Cursing solar power, I crawled out of the

city with the first of the rush-hour traffic. It was another hour before I made the Taconic and the beginning of freedom, and another after that before I arrived in the village. Out in the country, the sky was
robin's-egg blue, washed with lavender to the west,
and the long evening shadows dyed the early grass an
almost unimaginably deep emerald. No doubt that
brilliant bucolic charm would pale after a while—it
seemed to have worn thin on the film company—but
it lifted my spirits. I called the Delfs as soon as I
reached the village. Mr. Delf was dressing for dinner
and couldn't be disturbed. When I insisted, there was
a long pause while my message was conveyed. At
least I was told that he would see me after dinner. I
said I'd be along.

"That will be after nine," the butler added.

I made Independence Mutual pay for this delay
with a leisurely meal at The Huntsman. I picked up
some more gossip about the film company with my
veal marsala, then headed for the Delf estate. It was
a pleasant night, mild and a little damp, as if there'd
be rain before morning, and when I stopped the car
along the winding drive, I could hear peepers and
other frogs in the low meadows and the shallows of
the lake. From that angle, it did look like the water
where Dr. Kleinz had made his escape, and I thought
how odd it was that a fictional character could acquire
a personality, could even become a factor in one's
calculations. It was possible I was letting myself read
too much of Kleinz into the late Henry Brook, who
might have been a different sort of man altogether
from what I was imagining.

With this caution in mind, I proceeded up to the

house. I half expected Hector and the other dogs to
set up a row, but apparently they belonged to McNab,
for there were no signs of them. There were, however,
new tubs of flowers along the walk, and the windows
of the lower floor were brilliantly lit. When I rang the
bell, a short, dignified old gentleman with a seamed
and private face opened the door.

"Oh, yes, the insurance agent," he said when I
gave my name. "Please come in. Mr. Delf is just
finishing dinner. If you would like to sit in here."

He showed me into a small sitting room with good
but well-worn rugs and lots of pretty chintz. "Would
you like a cup of coffee? Mr. Delf is just finishing
his."

"Yes, please." He left like a shadow, and I had a
look around. There were lots of books, mostly fine
leather sets quite unmarred by use, several decent
nineteenth-century landscapes, and, on one table, a
number of family pictures. Within tortoiseshell and
silver frames, children sat splay-legged on fat Shet-
lands; a thin, rather homely boy piloted a sailboat,
and a portly man in tweeds posed with a gun and a
trophy. The caretaker had referred to young Mr. Delf.
I suspected he was the boy in the snap and guessed
from the look of the picture that he would be somewhere in his twenties. This supposition was confirmed
when the sailor, grown tall and carrying quite a bit of
added weight, appeared. Jim Delf was one of those
men who insist on doing several things at once. He
swept in with a drink in one hand and a cigarette in
the other and made a fuss over greeting me, parking
his cigarette in the corner of his mouth to shake my
hand.

"Has Hopkins gotten you a drink?"

"Some coffee, thank you."

"That's depressing. He always insists on coffee after dinner, no matter what I want."

The butler reappeared with a tray.

"Don't you?" Delf asked accusingly.

"Mrs. Delf always serves coffee after dinner," the man replied blandly. "Cream and sugar?"

"A little of each, please."

"You won't get me into that habit," Delf said. "Caffeine isn't healthy at all."

"There are worse habits, as you know, sir." The butler closed the doors behind him.

Delf had a sip of his drink and sniffed. "What kind of business are you in? Arthur mentioned you'd been by earlier."

"Independence Mutual held policies for both Henry Brook and for the picture. With such large sums, it is routine for us to make our own investigations. No reflection on any other work, just routine."

He gave a little cough that might have stifled a laugh. "You'll find the police and the medical staff here up to the minute on everything," he remarked sarcastically. "The very best the nineteenth century has to offer."

"That's small towns. They're not prone to experiment."

"Do you think so?" He squinted his pale eyes and scrunched his thin mouth. Young Mr. Delf was still rather homely, and he gave an impression of not having very much personality or wit. "I don't know. Other places seem reasonable. In the South, everyone seems reasonable. When I come back here, I'm always surprised to find everyone's an expert. Everyone knows just the way things should be done. There's nothing you can say.''

I nodded, attempting to be agreeable. His parents' old staff were probably not inclined to change their habits for him. As for the village...

"There's a certain feeling around that I got what I deserved.''

"You can't mean about—''

"Yes, of course, poor Henry Brook,'' he broke in. "I should never have brought those actors here.'' He nodded grimly. "It's medieval. Are you sure you wouldn't like a drink?''

"I'm fine, thank you.''

"Ironic.''

I wasn't sure if this referred to my abstemious habits or to the village's estimation of the actors. "Henry Brook was a personal friend of yours?'' I asked.

"Oh, yes, he knew my dad, actually. Uh-huh. Some investment deal years ago. He should have stuck with Dad. Father's a wizard with investments.''

"And Brook's own ideas weren't so inspired?''

"Well, his or Marylin's. Oh, they were fun. They did exciting things. Hotels in Guatemala, gold before it was legal, land schemes in the Amazon.''

"Fun is expensive.''

"Oh, absolutely. Father handled my portfolio.'' He gave a little sigh, nonetheless, as if, while sensible, he longed for panache and excitement.

"How did you get friendly with Henry Brook?''

"I met him years ago through Dad and then I got interested in the theater. I'd done some little things at

Yale—skits for a revue—and I thought Henry was a chance to get some ideas to the right people.''

''Did they?''

He looked up.

''Did your ideas get to the right people?''

''Not via Henry, I'm afraid.'' His mouth fell into a long, hard line. ''The whole business with the locations was a roundabout way to do that. I admired Rossol's work. That was how it came up. I was hinting how I'd like to meet Leonard Rossol—and talk about some of my ideas, of course...''

''Of course.''

''And Henry came up with the idea that we could use the estate and the Marsdens' place up the road for locations. It seemed a great idea.''

''On the scene, the house and the lake are very convincing. Very handsome.''

''No complaints about that.'' He sniffed again and sipped his drink. I revised his age up to the late twenties. There was something missing with him, some lack of satisfaction or purpose. Although he was surrounded with wealth and opportunity, I suspected that he had never quite made any of it pay off and that his enthusiasm for the movies had been shamelessly exploited by Brook and possibly by Rossol as well.

''What can you tell me about Henry Brook?'' I asked.

''He wasn't a man to do business with.''

''What do you mean?''

Delf took another drink and shifted his long legs as if even the large overstuffed chair was too small for him. ''Henry threw himself into everything. Mad enthusiasm. Excitement. Everything in a turmoil. While it suited him.''

"Aha."

"You know the type?"

I nodded.

"Then comes a change of mind."

"Goodbye enthusiasm."

"Right. Just about, in this case, as they were wrapping up the shooting here."

"While this…friendship…lasted, did you learn anything about him?"

"Oh, yes." He sipped his drink.

"Almost anything about his personality could be helpful to me," I hinted.

"I don't know that I feel like talking about him. It's after business hours. I come up here to relax."

"There's a great deal of money involved," I said, "even by your standards. There are certain unsatisfactory aspects of the case—due, as you correctly pointed out, to the conservative and antiquated procedures of this charming town. That is my problem. Your problem, I suspect, will turn out to be Marylin Brook.''

"God-awful woman."

"But reasonably smart and perhaps unreasonably greedy."

"How should that concern me?" he asked, but clearly it did now that it had been put to him.

"It's possible she might try to sue you for negligence, for inadequate upkeep of the dock where Henry fell, that sort of thing."

"She'd have no case."

"Don't be too sure. She could certainly make a fine

hullabaloo, and a sharp lawyer could make quite a nuisance of himself.''

"I doubt she has that kind of money. Not for a long haul.''

"But you've got enough to tempt a gamble. And your parents might not be keen on a lot of publicity. You might not be keen on their being disturbed. There are always possibilities, Mr. Delf.''

He shrank down into his chair with a sulky expression and finished his drink. "You really do need one of these,'' he said, meaning he needed drinking company. I agreed to a small scotch and nursed it as he put away several to a minimum effect.

"I know a lot about Henry. A lot of little things,'' he said, and with a sour face, he launched into a dissertation of the actor's faults and meannesses. Much I'd already learned in outline, but it came as news that Brook hadn't thought much of the *Lazarus* script and that he'd had a feud with Rossol going back several years.

"So why the party?'' I asked finally.

"Their idea—the film company's. A little thank-you for ruining the south lawn and rejecting my script.''

"Did you attend?''

"For a while. There were some fun people.'' His eyes brightened with the memory as if his life badly needed a little glitter.

"What kind of mood was Henry Brook in?''

"Same as always. But I didn't see much of him.''

"Any reason?''

"We'd had an argument the day before.''

"Something serious?''

"No, just another case of Henry's selfishness. It was a favor for Mummy, in fact. For her work with the Epilepsy Foundation."

"A favorite charity?"

"A little more than that. My stepbrother has grand mal. She's always contributed quite a lot to the foundation and naturally worried that the rest of us might develop it."

"I see. I'm sorry."

He lit another cigarette and seemed set to let the conversation die.

"What was it your mother wanted Henry to do?" I asked after a time.

"One of those commercial spots. You've perhaps heard them: they have a hockey player and a doctor and so on telling you they have the disease and how epilepsy can be controlled today."

"But Henry Brook didn't have epilepsy."

"That's where you're wrong. You don't necessarily foam at the mouth and fall down in convulsions, you know."

"I understand that, but..." There had been no mention of chronic disease in his medical report.

"Henry had a mild and rather rare kind. It got worse, though, as he'd gotten older. He told very few people. My folks knew because of Robbie's illness. I suppose he mentioned it one night in passing. I didn't know myself until a few weeks ago when Mummy asked me—"

"Yes, I see. Who else knew about this? His ex-wife, I'd imagine."

"Must have. She saw he took his medicine, doled

out his money—treated him like the infantile monster he was.''

''And Belinda?''

''Could have. She's a prying little tramp. Didn't miss much.''

''Anyone else besides them—and you?''

He sat upright. ''Really. I can't see the point of all this. The man's dead. What difference does it make who knew he had epilepsy? This might as well be the third degree.'' He leaned over and refilled his drink. ''What's happened to insurance agents?'' he asked jocularly. ''I liked the old kind—gray suit, button-down collar, carried big briefcases, didn't ask too many questions.''

''Old-fashioned insurance agents didn't cover multimillion-dollar movies.''

''Touché. Well, as far as I know, no one else knew. Part of Henry's vanity, you see. The glamorous, invulnerable star. Very macho.'' He laughed softly, as if reflecting on something amusing, which, indeed, he had been. ''That's why I told Rossol. He'd heard we'd had a fight and was in a snit: anything that might hold up the precious picture got him going. They were weeks late, as you probably know. I told him about Mummy and the Epilepsy Foundation because I knew it would bug Henry.''

''So Rossol knew Henry had epilepsy as well?''

''Yes. Tell the world as far as I'm concerned. It's not an unclean disease.''

''But surely you understand the implications.''

His face told me just as surely he didn't.

''Brook's death has not been satisfactorily explained,'' I said. ''There was the shallow water, the lack of any injury that could have rendered him unconscious. Epilepsy would explain how he fell, lost consciousness, drowned. Mr. Delf, you have straightened out the matter completely.''

''You don't know what you're talking about,'' he replied in a supercilious tone. ''Henry wasn't a grand mal or even a petit mal case. I told you he had a rare form.''

''I'm afraid you'll have to enlighten me.''

''Enlighten, yes. Enlighten. Lights, Ms. Insurance Investigator. Lights. Henry had a form of reflex epilepsy; he only lost consciousness in the presence of flashing lights.''

EIGHT

VALON WAS PLEASED. Indeed, given his usual dry, understated New England manner, I can say he was excited. Our phone conversation was punctuated by great rustlings of paper and calls for his secretary. "There's not a thing in the medical record," he exclaimed. "Not so much as a hint! Of course, we'll have to discuss this with Brook's private physician, but if we can confirm epilepsy, we'll be in quite a strong position for handling any claims."

"Several people without financial interests in either the policies or the picture knew about his condition."

"The Delfs, yes. They would be excellent witnesses. Not people to be suspected of bribery or collusion. I must congratulate you. A neat piece of work. You'll be going back to Washington today?"

"Yes, after the screening this morning."

"I'm not sure there's any need for that now," Valon said, thinking, no doubt, about my daily retainer.

"There may be. It's possible the doctor will claim confidentiality. The Delfs, while good witnesses, would not be as convincing as physical evidence."

"The perspective of a legalistic mind," Valon said, his good humor unruffled.

"I've just been thinking that the outtakes of the Berlin sequence might be revealing. There were a lot of explosions, smoke, flame, flashes of light. I'm not sure how Brook's illness affected him, but I know those scenes were frequently interrupted by his complaints of illness.''

"By all means, then, see the film, and I'll instruct Ed Martins to be sure nothing happens to the outtakes.''

"Good. And you'll check the medical angles?''

He said he would, and we hung up with unusually sincere expressions of esteem and satisfaction. I anticipated a large check from Independence Mutual and arrived at the screening room in an excellent mood. The projectionist was less congenial. He greeted me with a litany of complaints, which continued even after Brook appeared on the screen, stumbling from the garden of the Reich Chancellery with his face bloody. He managed a few steps, then stopped and put his hands over his face. Cut. Begin again. Hands over eyes was apparently too melodramatic. Another shot of Brook in Kleinz's costume and blood makeup, running through the smoke. There was a series of flashes to represent falling bombs, and he veered off his marks. Cut. A street scene with a dead horse and a starving family. Brook was in a medium shot, gasping for breath as he ran. A line of tracer bullets flashed overhead and the sky lit up as if from fireworks. Brook staggered a few more steps, then fell face forward. Cut. Cut. Cut. I could almost hear Rossol's uncomprehending fury. The string of outtakes continued. Stops, falls, odd, protective gestures that made me feel sadly omniscient: I was watching the destruction of a great actor whose vanity and arrogance had kept him from admitting that this splashy war drama was literally making him sick.

It had started, Belinda had said, like a game. A little

tension on the set. A director pulling rank, making unfair criticisms or refusing to give in on the trifles that sway so much of human conduct. An actor goofing off, arriving late, stepping on someone else's lines, or refusing to learn his own: "a contemptible little Nazi charade" had been Brook's assessment of the script, according to Jim Delf. And then, just at the wrong moment, came the director's centerpiece, the spectacular destruction of Berlin, complete with the ruined Nazi Chancellery and the Brandenburg Gate, obscenely expensive and lit by enough current to brown out Manhattan. With the picture already behind schedule, the money people would have been getting nervous, especially after the rumormongers began tapping out "items": "Big Budget *Lazarus Gambit* in Trouble?", "Delays Threatening Rossol Studio Gamble?", "Feud Rumored on *Lazarus Gambit* Set." It was easy to see how things had turned sour.

In the next sequence, Brook had reached the gate, and his exhaustion was all too realistic. The shot caught him looking toward where the Russian troops were supposed to be, and, as the bombs began flashing, he cringed and passed his hand over his eyes.

"What the hell is this? Who authorized those outtakes? If this is your idea of a joke, Len, you can speak to my lawyer." It was Marylin Brook and she didn't sound happy.

"Oh, for God's sake, Marylin! Joe, Joe! What the fuck's going on here? I didn't tell you to set that up. Now, listen, Marylin—" Len Rossol saw me stand up down front and stopped short. "Ms. Peters."

"Hello, Mr. Rossol, Mrs. Brook, Belinda," I said, but it was no time for pleasantries. Marylin Brook had a temper like a rhino, and Rossol wasn't doing much to settle her down.

At this point, the projectionist banged out of his booth, all sweetness and light as usual, and a great deal of high-decibel conversation ensued. Meanwhile Brook lurched away from the Brandenburg Gate, while bombs whined and bullets hit the dust, putt-putt-putt. Then Marylin stalked up to the booth, screaming that she was going to rip the film out. The projectionist was describing what would befall her if she touched the smallest dial on his equipment, when Belinda, who had a cooler head than I'd credited, found the overhead light switch. Berlin became a washed-out pastel, and the angry group around the projectionist's booth had a surprised moment to regain their composure.

"You can switch that off now, Joe," I said. "Apparently there was some scheduling mistake."

Marylin began to describe just what our respective errors were, but I pointed out that as Independence Mutual's representative, I was entitled to examine all the footage, including outtakes.

"You vultures," Marylin burst out. "You should remember him at his best. Not by a lot of trashy footage in a second-rate thriller."

"That's not what you said at *The Lazarus Gambit* signing, Marylin, dear," Rossol snapped. "Henry had his days...and his days." He jerked his chin toward the projectionist. "Put on our other reels, Joe. I tried to get you last night, Anna. We had to switch screenings, because I'm supposed to fly to the Coast. I hope you don't mind."

"What are you going to show?" I asked. Having

discovered what Independence Mutual needed, I could afford to be obliging.

"Some of the Argentina scenes. You're welcome to watch. There's nothing salvageable in that Berlin footage anyway. We've taken everything useful." He checked his watch, then asked casually, "Where were you last night? I kept calling until after midnight."

"I was upstate and didn't get back until late."

"Upstate?" He covered his surprise and interest with a joke. "I didn't know insurance people were so fond of the country. What's going on up there?"

That was none of his business. "You should have left a message," I said, "but that's all right. I can watch the reels you want to see."

But nothing was right as far as Marylin was concerned, and there were another five minutes of recriminations. During this tirade, I whispered to Joe that Ed Martins would be along for the outtakes, and Gloria arrived in a fluster with her notebook, apologizing for being late. "Such traffic. I should have stayed at the other hotel. I'm not sure separating the crew was such a good idea after all," she began, but Rossol gave her a look and she shut up.

"No luck for her," Belinda whispered slyly to me, as Rossol and Marylin went into an intense huddle with the others. "She's been banished to the Sheraton. I think he's seeing Lani. Very convenient, with her play opening Off Broadway."

"What's this get-together for, anyway?"

"Haven't you heard? I thought the insurance company would have been the first informed," Belinda said. "You sure you're on the level?"

"Don't play games. You may need me later."

She made a face. "It's a tribute to Henry. There's some good footage for television. A prime-time special on the filming of *The Lazarus Gambit*, exploiting the tragedy to the hilt, of course. Too bad the drowning wasn't on film," she added bitterly. "It would have made the perfect climax for them."

She sat down by herself in a corner of the screening room, until Rossol went over and teased her into joining the group. Then he yelled for lights out. The big projector hummed into life, and I sat down next to Gloria. Marylin settled herself directly in front of us, and Rossol kept leaning over to explain to her how whatever we were seeing could be cut to fit the proposed documentary. He had adopted a conciliatory, almost cajoling tone with her that was so uncharacteristic I decided she must have a veto over anything to do with the late actor's work.

"Voice-over," said Marylin. "Who's doing that?"

"I thought I would," said Rossol. "Now this East River stuff, him getting off the boat—might show how we used the New York locations, might get an angle there."

"I thought we'd try for a big name," Marylin said. "Someone like Newman; they were friends. It would add some class. And I'd like to do some of it too."

"Maybe on some of the personal stuff, Marylin. For the rest—yeah, a name actor. But I like Robards, a great voice."

"Little less expensive, maybe."

"Course, if I do it myself, that adds another dimension. We don't have the back-country stuff shot. Maybe we could fly a camera crew out to location for the opening: 'Henry Brook was supposed to come to this village on the edge of the Argentine pampas, but he never made it.'''

"Expensive," remarked Marylin.

"Yeah, maybe."

Altheia Karl appeared on the screen, her blonde glamour somewhat subdued by a severe coiffeur and a plain gray dress that emphasized a resemblance to Evita Peron. She carried a shopping bag and a box tied with thin string, which she deposited in a sunny kitchen. Kleinz was in the bedroom, sleeping on top of the covers. The doctor had aged considerably since his last appearance in Berlin and had added a short mustache. As he slept, the muscles in his face twitched and his thin, sensitive mouth twisted into an expression of anguish.

"We'd planned to cut in some flashbacks for his dream—something from the camp or the visit to Himmler," Rossol remarked. "I hadn't quite decided which."

The man on the bed gave a soft cry and sat up abruptly, his gray face damp with sweat, his eyes startled. When he saw Altheia, his shoulders slumped, and he ran a weary hand over his eyes.

"Another dream?" she asked.

Kleinz shook his head. "I can't remember. It wouldn't be so bad if I could only remember." His remarkable eyes were stricken; the detachment that had characterized the doctor in the earlier reels had been replaced by an intense, puzzled sorrow, and even in this rough cut the change was strikingly effective.

Altheia came to the bed to comfort him. One thing led to another, and before long the pair were gracefully entwined, tawny hair and golden skin against the white sheets and amber shadows of the southern afternoon.

"Best tits in the business," Rossol sighed.

"Too Virgin Queen," said Marylin, who obviously envisioned her own grieving-widow performance holding center stage. "She doesn't belong on the screen with Henry; I've heard better lines at amateur night."

I thought that was a little unfair. Altheia Karl had assessed her talent fairly accurately. Her range was small, but her grace and her brilliant looks suited erotic material. Quite without vulgarity, she produced a very classy bedroom scene.

"If you leave all that in," Belinda said, "you'd better hope it goes on HBO."

"Cut for the domestic networks," Rossol said. "What's up next, Gloria?"

"The hospital scenes."

We saw Kleinz examining an emaciated old man.

"Cut in a memory of the camp here," Rossol said. "Very quick. The girl's body, maybe, the rib cage, a different kind of white light."

"I'm going to be famous," Belinda said.

"Best ribs in the business," Rossol teased.

"Last ribs to appear with Henry Brook!" she exclaimed. She had Lani's intonation down pat.

Rossol turned businesslike. "We have that, Gloria? We have that shot listed?"

"Take four, camp scene five, subject's death."

"Same side? He on her right? They've got to match for full effect."

"I'll check, but I'm sure it's a match, and he was using his stethoscope, too."

"Okay, we'll want that. We can use this one as well."

"There will be a difference in light levels," Gloria warned. "There's nothing this bright in the camp shots, not with that yellowish green lighting you used."

She did not have to consult her notes for this, and I was impressed with her memory. Rossol, so snappish and supercilious on all other matters, never questioned her accuracy. How unfortunate the police had not made more use of that trained recall! Believing she was a minor and unimportant member of the crew, they had asked her only the briefest and most perfunctory questions, and Gloria, who struck me as unusually agreeable and docile, had not pushed herself forward in any way.

"God, I hate to see this," Rossol exclaimed. "If we had put this together the right way, they'd have been on the edge of their seats. We could even have let the frigging African prologue go, if we'd only had the exterior Latin shots."

Rossol turned to me. I was getting VIP treatment. "We used Delf's other house for this next sequence. That great barn of a hunting lodge is perfect home-sick-kraut architecture. We got several of the right kind of rooms. Then we cut to a chase we did here. Found a neighborhood that looked right and brought in some palms and stuff. The Argentine government is still kind of sensitive about any picture with a political angle, so we were keeping the Latin footage to the bare minimum."

The projector started up again.

"Yeah, here we go," Rossol said. "The doc's leaving his patient for a little cigarette break."

In a dim, rather cramped hallway, a match flared, lighting the doctor's drawn but still handsome face. While Belinda whispered flirtatiously with Rossol, we watched Brook explore a well-sandbagged stairway into the basement of the house. At the bottom was a door and behind the door were a hospital bed, oxygen equipment, an IV rack. The camera swept over these things, mimicking Kleinz's frantic, horrified recognition, revealed cooling equipment, pumps, and tubing, and, finally, in a swift ninety-degree turn, a man on the bed. It was Adolf Hitler.

"I think if we had some voice-over, this could go in," Marylin said.

"Over the footage? You want to spoil the effect? Marylin, sweetheart! God! This is the craft of suspense laid out for you. You want a voice-over? You want to kill it? Is this classic or isn't this classic? Guilt, flashback, recognition, a trap, an escape, another trap; it's building all the time, baby. And at the end, the doctor's smashing the guy's head—total instinctive, automatic act. The animal's loose. You've got to love it."

"Yes," said Marylin in a dry, cynical tone. "Love's the word. A bit of a temptation for you, Len."

"What do you mean, Marylin?"

"To shoot it all again."

"Sweetheart! The cast, the crew, the money—all gone."

"Yes?"

"Yes, goddamn it."

"That's why you just happen to be going to the Coast, rush, rush, to talk to Redford's agent?"

"Oh, Christ! Marylin!"

"Don't you bullshit me, Len," Marylin shouted. "You try to cut me out and you'll have trouble."

They exchanged some inventive profanity on this subject, but by insisting he only wanted to suggest the narration to Redford, Rossol eventually produced a stalemate, if not a reconciliation.

"Marylin's a little overwrought," he said to me on the way out. "A hard time for her."

Down in the tatty lobby, Marylin had a word of her own. "Don't give that son of a bitch his money too soon," she said. "I wouldn't trust him for a minute."

NINE

I RETURNED TO WASHINGTON, and *The Lazarus Gambit* came to rest on my office shelf. If I had doubts or questions, I put them aside. Valon was satisfied; the company had seized the incomplete medical statement as their loophole and lawyers for both sides were preparing to profit. I had other work, other problems. Among other things, tight money teaches you to take a professional approach.

It may be, though, that a certain residual uneasiness remained. On two separate evenings I carted the novel home, astonished that with Hitler hidden, Kleinz disguised, heroines altered, and eight hundred pages behind him, our indefatigable author still had nearly twenty chapters to go. I was wondering how he would manage when the Israelis provided an answer. As Kleinz fled, with the Nazi goons behind him, three stalwarts from Tel Aviv appeared, summoned urgently by their colleague, Agent Butterfly. A few chapters later, I found the party scene Altheia Karl had so enthusiastically described and was disillusioned to discover that the butterfly pin and the mystery of her identity were both elaborations conceived by Len Rossol.

I began to appreciate the mass of verbiage that Rossol had reduced to film. One hundred pages of close-set type were devoted to the search for the hibernation capsule before the novel's focus shifted to the Nazis, who were busy planning a rally where the talisman of talismans would be revealed: an appearance by the revivified Adolf Hitler.

"How're you doing with that?" Harry asked. He was sitting on the couch with his feet up, quietly making sketches.

"I don't know why I'm bothering to read it, but I'm closing in on the big Nazi rally. I assume that's where we'll have a splashy denouement."

"Right you are. Everyone shows up. Too bad about Rossol's picture. He would have done something super with the conclusion."

"Yes, hard luck."

"Continuing, too. Did you see the *Times* today?"

"No, what happened?"

"Wait a minute. Did I bring my copy home?" Harry got up and went to look, returning a moment later with the paper. "Yes, here it is. I was checking the galleries in New York when it caught my eye. 'Upstate Village Sees Bad Luck Continuing.'"

The story was buried in the paper's amorphous second section, a little piece picked up by a local stringer. I saw the Delf name and quickly skimmed the column. "...blaming bad luck on the recent filming of *The Lazarus Gambit*. Actor Henry Brook drowned earlier this month in an accident on location at the estate of the Jahred H. Delfs. Villagers see the latest incident, an attack on the estate caretaker, Arthur McNab, 63, as evidence.... McNab, a native of Inverness, Scotland...trained dog handler and gardener...struck by an unknown assailant late Friday afternoon in one of the outbuildings of the sprawling estate north of town. Villagers uneasy...blame presence of actors and outsiders.... McNab, unconscious for several hours, expected to recover...life saved by the barking of his bull mastiff, Hector, a familiar figure about the small town.''

Suppressed doubts came into focus. ''I'm going to have to go up there,'' I said. ''And I'd better call Independence Mutual, too. Police first, I suppose, though who'll be on duty in the village at this hour, I don't know. The state police probably.''

''What are you talking about? I thought that was finished and wrapped up. You said the insurance people were exceptionally pleased.''

''I did and they were. Unless I'm wrong, this changes everything.''

''Go on, what's the connection? He was probably running around on his wife, and she clobbered him.''

''Not in an outbuilding, she wouldn't. Besides, country people have guns. McNab was carrying a twenty-two the day I met him. If she'd been serious, she'd have shot him.''

''Feminine indecision,'' Harry teased.

''Baloney. This is a town where trouble on a Saturday night means a kid chucking a beer can, and 'that's since the new plant opened in the Valley'—I quote the coroner. Within three weeks one of the biggest stars in America dies in the lake and the caretaker on the same spread is nearly murdered. Hand me the phone book, would you?''

''He's not going to like this,'' my sensible husband said.

''Who?''

''Your insurance man.''

"Probably not. But there's a possibility they didn't want to consider."

"What's that?"

"That Henry Brook was murdered."

"Well, they won't like it any better now. They'd have to pay upon the claim then, wouldn't they?"

"That would depend on who killed him."

"Oh."

"I can probably find out. And if I do, I think I'll raise the subject with Independence Mutual—at something above my usual fee, of course."

"Is that why you're going? I thought you were out of the woods, financially speaking."

I realized that my fiscal difficulties had been on his mind. Graphic work wasn't booming either at the moment, and neither of us wanted to be in debt to his prosperous but mercurial partner. "Pretty much so. Thanks to that Independence Mutual check. But I like Mr. McNab. He's the chatty sort that appeals to me, and he's as harmless an old gaffer as you could find. There's got to be a reason."

"But not necessarily one Independence Mutual will pay for," Harry said.

I wished he hadn't reminded me. "Maybe not, but Mrs. Brook is a Tartar. She'll go to court if she's not paid in full, which she doesn't deserve if Brook lied on his medical forms. She's trouble and a half and smart enough to make the same kind of connections I have. Valon and the company better have their facts straight if they're going to war with her."

"So you get a trip north?"

"Think of it as venture capitalism," I said and went to sit on the arm of the couch. "Tell you what.

Call and make my reservations; I'll talk to the police, and then we'll have a little time to ourselves."

"The sort of proposition I always like," Harry said, putting his arm around me. "But remember, if you come home with bruises, we're not on speaking terms."

I REACHED THE VILLAGE at one the next afternoon, having been delivered from the tender mercies of our national rail system to the last car available at the rental agency in Poughkeepsie. In this resplendent yellow sedan I rolled up to the diner, where I had a quick lunch and made some phone calls before pressing on to the hospital. I arrived near the start of visiting hours, and when I inquired about Arthur McNab, a short, compact woman with red hair and a thin, sharp face appeared out of the crowded waiting room.

"What would you be wanting with Arthur McNab?"

"Mrs. McNab?" I guessed. "I'm Anna Peters. If I could have a word with you, please."

"We've had police. We've had state police. We've had reporters from *The New York Times.* I said to Arthur, I said, it's a painful way to become a celebrity. Now I think we've had enough. And him lying there with his head aching. He's too soft, that's what he is."

That failing was not evident in his consort. "Perhaps we could step outside," I said, aware of the stares of the lethargic waiting-room crowd. "It's very important. I came up from Washington this morning."

Mrs. McNab glanced around the room as if calling

the others to witness the irregularity of the proceedings before her curiosity got the better of her. "I'll be back presently, miss," she told the receptionist. Then, with a glance that dared me to try anything funny, she pushed out the doors, past tardy visitors clutching anxiety and potted plants. When we reached the parking lot, she said, "Well, Miss Peters, what's your business?"

"I interviewed your husband last week for Independence Mutual Insurance, the company that holds the insurance policies for both the film company that was at the Delf estate and for the late Henry Brook."

"Arthur mentioned you'd been by."

"When I read in the paper that your husband had been injured, I felt it was vital that I speak to him again. And perhaps important for his safety."

"His safety? It doesn't seem your first visit did much for that."

"That's precisely it, Mrs. McNab. I'm beginning to think there may have been a connection."

"What do you mean?"

"Although I was working for Independence Mutual, I own my own investigation agency. The insurance company called on me because they were not satisfied with the explanations for Henry Brook's drowning."

"That was ruled misadventure. Will Keegan's been coroner here for thirty years," she added, though whether this long tenure was a point in his favor, I could not tell.

"The incident with your husband—"

"He was nearly murdered. I don't call that much of an 'incident,'" she said, but the tartness was going out of her. She was clearly worried. "I don't want him bothered. I don't want him worried."

"Certainly not," I said, though from my observation of Arthur McNab, I suspected he would be dying for some diversion. "But if he's able, I think it would be wise to let me talk to him. He didn't strike me as a man who'd appreciate being left in the dark about anything important."

"Oh, you're right about that. Nor out of anything unimportant, either." She sighed. "Knowing what to do is an awful bother."

"Mrs. McNab, is there anyone in the village who might have done such a thing? Anyone with a grudge against your husband?"

"No, no. Arthur's a well-liked man. One of the best liked in the village and no exaggeration. Why, the calls I've had. And flowers, cards, pots of spaghetti, cakes." She stopped and wiped her eyes. "He's a man everyone likes."

"My impression as well. So, Mrs. McNab, if it wasn't someone from the village, it was some stranger. And there's only been one group of strangers lately, and those were the movie people."

"I don't know why they ever had to allow that lot in the first place. Such a carrying-on we had with them. You'd have thought Arthur was working for them. 'Oh, Arthur, would you just run us here or there?' Why, some nights he wasn't finished till after ten and then they'd think nothing of ringing up at the crack of dawn. They did get up early, I'll say that for them. That Miss Tayana was the worst one. Always wanting something. Most likely something she shouldn't have, if you ask me."

"Belinda?"

"That's her name. A model, she said she was. Desperate to go to Poughkeepsie. Though what there was for her there, I'm sure I don't know."

I didn't know either. "Did Mr. McNab ever take her in?"

"Oh, every Friday when he went for the errands, she'd be there. And she was always after him to make a trip special, but he just had to tell her he was working for the Delfs, not their guests."

"Quite right." I took out one of my cards and wrote a message. "Perhaps you could give him this and ask if he feels well enough to talk."

She took it, then shook her head. "Never mind. Come away. If Arthur once sees this, he'll be out of bed. How I'll get him to rest when he's so bored, I don't know."

"I'll be there in five minutes," I said, thinking she might want to speak to him first, and she must have appreciated this, for I was greeted cordially upstairs. The caretaker was sitting in bed with his head bandaged. There was a grayish tinge to his weathered face, and his eyes had the strained look that comes from pain, shock, and hospital dope. "I didn't believe Kit when she said you'd come all the way back. I thought she was pulling my leg."

"How are you, Mr. McNab?" His hand was leathery and strong and his bare forearm well muscled. Although slight, he would not have been the easiest victim.

"Another day in bed, they say."

"If he can only get some rest," his wife added.

"Rest! I'm sick of this resting. It's for the concussion, you know. They watch me and want me to rest, but they keep waking me up.''

We commiserated on this, then I asked about Hector, and McNab's face glowed. "A brave pup that. Bred him myself, raised him from the time he was weaned. He saved my life.''

"How did it happen? I'm sorry to trouble you again, but the papers were rather vague.''

"It's no trouble. My wife tells me you're a private investigator.''

"Yes. You are welcome to check on that if you wish.''

"I knew you were after something the first time you came. I said to my wife—didn't I, Kit?''

"That's right, Arthur, so you did.''

"It's just as well, isn't it? This''—he gestured toward his wounded head—''was a very odd thing.''

"That's why I wasted no time, Mr. McNab. Your injury has got to be connected to Brook's drowning. You must know something, or else someone mistakenly thinks you do. Either way, we ought to try to find out what and who.''

He nodded and took a sip of water from the cup beside his bed.

"If you could, I'd like you to go through your usual Friday routine. I understand you made regular trips into Poughkeepsie?''

"The Delfs do their daily shopping here in the village, but there were certain things that they can get only in town. Mr. Delf, that's young Mr. Delf now, likes to read some foreign papers. They come into the big newsstand on a Friday. And they buy their liquor in Poughkeepsie—a little falling-out they had with the local man a number of years ago.''

''Did you go in at any set time?''

''Well, never in the mornings—the train with the papers doesn't arrive until early afternoon. I usually leave around two and return shortly after four.''

We talked about this for a time and about Belinda Tayana and her trips into town. I gathered there was a boy involved and lost interest. What was clear was that Mr. McNab's routine was regular and well known. It would also have been known that Hector, otherwise his invariable companion, was left at home on these junkets into the big town.

''This past Friday,'' I asked, ''what time did you get home?''

''Four-thirty, maybe even four-forty-five, because of the extra traffic.''

''What traffic was that?''

''Parents weekend at the college down the road. They come in from all over, and, of course, there's no where much to park in the village or around the campus.''

How unfortunate, I thought. Ordinarily a strange car would have stood out like a fire engine.

''Well, I drove up to the stable. That's—what? a hundred yards, would you say, Kit? from our place. I got out, opened the door, pulled the car in. Hector was barking. I should say I'd left him in one of the stalls because Kit was to be working up at the big house all afternoon. When young Mr. Delf is away she takes the dog up with her, but not when Mr. Delf is home because he doesn't like dogs.''

''Was it unusual for Hector to be barking?''

McNab considered this. "He'll bark when I come in, but yes, it was. I just assumed it was a rat somewhere. I was thinking I'd have to bring up Trig, that's the wee terrier you saw, and try to flush the vermin out."

I nodded. "Then what?"

"I opened the car. I'd had to get supplies—nails and boxes of screws for some repair work I need to do. I thought I'd unload them and let Hector out before I took the rest of the messages up to the main house."

"You still had the liquor in the car and the other shopping?"

"Oh, yes. Several hundred dollars' worth."

"And none of this was taken?"

"No."

So it wasn't a robbery attempt or any casual, opportunistic crime.

"As I say, I pulled the car in," McNab continued, "and took out the bag with the nails and such. Hector was barking and growling up a storm and I hollered for him to quiet down. Never thinking, you know. I came around the car, crossed toward the bench, heard something, then bingo. I was hit; I feel this big"— he lifted his hands and brought them together as if to illustrate the sudden blow. "That's all. The next thing I remember was Hector barking and licking my face and Kit hammering on the door outside."

"How did Hector get loose?"

"He busted off the latch. Those old stalls are pretty well shot. The door was secured with a light sliding catch. He must have been working on it for a while, lunging at the door, and finally it gave."

"Did he get hold of your assailant, do you think?"

"If Hector'd gotten hold of him, he'd be there still. No, I think whoever it was saw the door start to give, panicked, ran outside, and closed the overhead garage door. That was put in just recent and once it was down, he was safe. Hector kept up a row until Kit came along, wondering why I hadn't showed up at the house and heard him."

That was right, I thought later, standing in the soft gloom of the stable. Following McNab's directions, I had found the old fieldstone structure easily. Set among overgrown paddocks, it had a wooden loft, a steep slate roof, and a new aluminum sliding door that led to the open area once used for grooming horses. To my right were rows of stalls, dusty and neglected except for the nearest, which was clean and floored with woodchips. There was an old rug, a pan for water, and a smooth, well-gnawed knuckle bone: Hector's domain. As McNab said, the catch on the outside of the stall had proved weak. Inside the stall I inspected the other side of the door. Hector had obviously spent considerable time trying to escape, for his nails had gouged through to the white wood beneath the old dark paint, and the scratches were almost all fresh. The assailant had come to the stable ahead of time and hidden. Probably he—or possibly she—had not expected the dog to be there but had been confident that the animal was secured. I suspected, too, that the attacker had been unarmed; someone with a gun would most likely have dispatched the dog. But Hector was too large and fierce to tackle without some very substantial weapon, and I could imagine the discomfort of waiting, hidden in the recesses of the stable, listening to the mastiff's attempts to escape.

I returned to the entry. There was an irregular oblong of grease where McNab habitually parked his car, then, to the left, a series of small rooms, where originally the grooms would have stored their tack and equipment and slept. One was fitted out as a small workshop, which I was puzzled to notice was in disarray. McNab seemed a careful workman: this was evident in the neat rows of tools mounted on the wall, the plastic trays labeled with the dimensions of various nails and screws, the lumber stacked in piles by width below the bench. But someone had had a good rummage. A keg of nails had been tipped over on the floor, various boxes of fuses, washers, tape, and hardware had been dumped out on the work surface. While I wondered why, I went back to examine the inner surface of the garage door. Again, NcNab's theory seemed correct: although the new metal was much more resistant than the ancient stable doors, there were a host of marks and scratches as well as a few muddy dog prints. The assailant had hidden, it appeared, in one of the many dark alcoves formed by the warren of tack rooms on the left side of the building. Mcnab pulled the car in, got out, and went to the back to remove his supplies. The assailant waited until he entered the corridor to his workshop, then struck him from behind. Here things became unclear. Had the blow been intended to kill, stun, or frighten? To stun I thought unlikely unless, surprised in his examination of the workshop, the intruder had struck McNab in order to escape. It was possible that the aim had been to frighten the caretaker. In that case, the attacker could have departed before Hector broke loose. The third possibility was the most sinister. McNab had been struck but not finished off because the big, powerful dog had broken out of the stall and necessitated a swift retreat. Possible? I ran up the door, then jerked it down to see how quickly it would shut but came to no firm conclusion. Though, like most garage overheads, the door was a bit stiff, it was possible that someone who was nervous around dogs would have bolted at the first crack of the wood, or that Hector would have run to his injured master before attacking the intruder.

Next I made a careful survey of the workshop: McNab apparently doubled as the estate handyman, for there was a complete supply of hardware: locks, knobs, latches, bolts, sashcord, screening, nails, screws, and hooks and eyes in dozens of different types and sizes, as well as fuses, washers, weather-stripping, putty. Everything had been messed together as if hasty hands had muddled through the stuff, and as I walked around, my feet rattled the nails and bolts that had fallen to the floor along with the sawdust and wood scraps tipped from the waste bin. What had McNab's visitor been looking for? I got down on my hands and knees to begin sifting through the debris, but I had found nothing more suggestive than a few flat washers and a broken light bulb when I heard a rattle at the back of the stable, followed by a single footstep and the unpleasant silence of someone listening hard. I straightened up quietly and slid one of McNab's large wrenches into easier reach on the bench. In the seconds that followed, I was painfully aware of the isolation of the estate and the thicknesses of the walls of the stable. I knew I had lowered the garage door. That meant my visitor had entered through one of the locked doors to the rear, which suggested—

"Is anyone there?" a man called. I recognized Jim Delf's voice.

The light was on; my car was only half concealed behind the McNab's cottage. I had no choice but to answer.

"Yes, it's Anna Peters."

Delf appeared in the doorway, obviously surprised and, from his expression, unlikely to play the gracious host for this meeting. I had time, too, to remember both his dislike of dogs and his quarrel with Henry Brook, before I managed a disingenuous smile and that air of brightness that men frequently mistake for simplemindedness. "Hello, I'm sorry to intrude, but I'd come to talk to Arthur McNab and couldn't resist a look. It was such a shock, wasn't it?"

"I'd prefer, in the future, if you'd check with me first, Ms. Peters." He spoke in a huffy tone, but I thought I detected relief. He had been carrying a large flashlight, which he set down somewhat sheepishly on the workbench. "Someone's made a fine mess of this," he said, glancing at me.

"Whoever struck Mr. McNab, I suppose, unless the police raked through this stuff."

"I don't believe so. I'll have a word with the constable in any case." Although he frowned and stalked around with his nose in the air, Jim Delf found it hard to maintain the pose of outraged property owner, and I soon discovered that his chief anxiety was his parents' anger. But beyond confirming McNab's story and his popularity in the village, he told me little of importance until I was set to leave.

"You'll excuse me for not saying I hope to see you again," he said by way of farewell.

"It's understandable. I don't suppose you're eager to see any of the people involved with the picture."

"I'm eager to avoid them," he said. "Especially Len and Marylin."

"Have you been in touch with them?"

"Oh, yes. They've been pestering me for the past week. Both of them would like a loan, but neither wants to come right out and say—"

"I thought Rossol had been away. He was leaving for California last I heard."

"Canceled that, or rather postponed it. Something came up. He's away now, I think. Marylin calls regularly. In fact, she called me from Poughkeepsie the day Arthur was hurt."

"What time was that?" I asked quickly.

"Early afternoon. Something with Belinda, I think. Why she was up, I mean. Don't look like that. Why would she have wanted to hurt poor old Arthur? Even Marylin's romantic entanglements are not that complicated." He gave a nervous little laugh.

I agreed it was a nonsensical thought, but I decided that as soon as I got back to the city, I would find out exactly how Rossol, Mrs. Brook, and Belinda had spent Friday afternoon.

TEN

I REACHED NEW YORK with some relief. There was something about the estate that was too nicely calculated: the outbuildings were too quaint, the woods too thick, the privileges of the main house too evident. The twilight city had beauties of its own but no fewer questions, as I discovered when I began the job of tracing the recent whereabouts of Henry Brook's ex-wife, girlfriend, and director.

Belinda's modeling agency was, of course, closed, and there was no answer from the Greenwich Village townhouse. After Rossol's hotel revealed that he was away in California and not expected back for two days, I gave up, phoned Harry, and went to bed early. The next morning a new, or should I say an old, character made her appearance. In the guise of a rather dim secretary, I began calling every contact I could think of for my three suspects and was pleased to find that a certain glib facility for lying had not entirely deserted me during a stretch of clean living.

By midmorning I was satisfied that Len Rossol had indeed been in the state until last Saturday, giving him time to attack McNab. I also learned that Belinda had canceled several appointments the previous Friday, thus removing her soundest alibi. Mrs. Brook proved a tougher case. When I visited her house, the bell went unanswered and the next-door neighbors proved uncooperative. Momentarily stymied, I found a street

vendor, risked a hotdog with all the fixings, and settled in the nearby park to keep an eye on the house.
About an hour later I was rewarded when Belinda
emerged, dressed in a pair of dark slacks and a white
sweater. When she was too close to avoid me, I
stepped around the hedge at the side of the park. Like
Jim Delf, she did not seem particularly pleased.

"Oh, it's you. I thought you'd gone back to the
home office or whatever." She waved her hand, displaying beautifully tended red nails.

"Well, I thought everything was settled," I replied,
as chatty as could be, "but everything's in an uproar
again. I'm sure you understand."

She looked puzzled.

"The attack on the caretaker—you'd heard about
that, hadn't you?"

"What caretaker?"

"At the Delfs."

"Not Arthur. He was so nice! Not obliging," she
added judiciously, "but nice. What happened to
him?"

"Someone hit him over the head with the prover-
bial blunt instrument. He's lucky to be alive."

"When? When was this?"

"Last Friday."

Belinda's expression turned anxious. "You're kid-
ding! It's not true!"

"Check the Monday *Times*. Of course, that
changes everything, don't you think?" I rattled on,
watching her expression. "I admit your theory did not
impress me at first but now I'm reconsidering."

"What are you talking about?" Belinda asked. She

really was surprised; her normally quick reactions were slowed.

"Someone wants to keep Arthur McNab from telling what he knows, wouldn't you think? And what would he know? That Henry Brook killed himself? Marylin certainly wouldn't care to have that spread about. Or maybe that Henry Brook was killed by someone? You suggested yourself—"

"Stop it!" Belinda said, stamping her foot and clenching both fists. "Stop it! Don't say that about Marylin. She had nothing to do with it. Nothing!"

"You gave me the idea." I fell into step as she began to stride away. "Marylin had a motive for her husband's death. In the case of Mr. McNab, she had both motive and opportunity, since she was up in Poughkeepsie the day it happened."

Belinda stopped again, shocked. "How did you know about that?"

"Knowing is my business," I said. Delf had not lied; Marylin had been upstate.

"It wasn't for that," Belinda said and, to my surprise, tears came to her eyes. "It wasn't for that at all."

"But can she prove it? And where were you, Belinda?"

"We weren't in the village," she replied angrily. "Never. It had nothing to do with Henry or anyone else. Nothing at all."

I started to say something else, but Belinda screamed, "Leave me alone! Leave me alone right now!" attracting the attention of even the blasé Village habitués as she darted across the street toward the subway entrance. I decided not to follow; she had already given me plenty to think about. Instead, I spent the afternoon entertaining some past and prospective clients and trying to keep up with my neglected office work via long distance. In the early evening I managed to reach Arthur McNab, newly released from the hospital and sounding tired and rather groggy. He could not think of anything valuable that might have been in his workshop, nor could he remember the film company's reporting anything lost or stolen. He would "sleep on it," he promised, and would call me if anything came to mind.

That was the best I could expect, but after I hung up the phone, I began to wander restlessly around my hotel room. I had sixteen or eighteen hours before I could reasonably hope to contact Rossol and, while I might try to catch Marylin Brook, I doubted I'd learn very much from her.

Below my window, bright squiggles of neon cut into the blue evening and the traffic surged with a steady roar like surf. I was bored stiff; the filtered, chemically tainted hotel air, the semiabstract landscape over the bed, my briefcase stuffed with half-read papers—all the tedious accoutrements of business travel were suddenly repugnant. I would dress up and go to dinner, I thought, then corrected myself. I would use the hotel pool, then eat somewhere really elegant. Pleased with this idea, I unpacked my suit and had kicked off my shoes when there was a knock. "Just a minute."

Again.

"A minute," I repeated.

I opened the door, but the corridor was empty, and although I heard footsteps, no one was in evidence

except two men waiting by the elevator. A mistake
perhaps. I returned to my room, changed, and went
down ten floors to the pool, which was set below a
terrace equipped with wrought-iron chairs and tables
for fashion shows and private parties. At one end of
the room was a row of changing cubicles and at the
other more tables and a sitting area, plus an office for
the lifeguard. Along the remaining side ran a glass-
sided and roofed deck, for those who fancied sun-
bathing six floors above Manhattan. The sign at the
door said the pool closed in another half hour, and
only a couple of shivering kids sat huddled in towels
on the deck, while a man and a woman swam slow
laps in the pool. I bundled up my clothes, slid into
the aquamarine water, and began stroking rhythmi-
cally up and down the short lanes. As always when
swimming, various problems that I had been working
on flowed in and out of focus in a pleasantly detached
manner. Maybe it is the partial escape from gravity
that robs problems of their urgency when considered
in water, but in any case, I was content to let one idea
after another float through my mind. Presently the
other swimmers left, the couple padding wetly across
the fake grass on the terrace and talking noisily about
some plans for later that evening. The children departed next, hurried away by their overdressed mama.
Shortly afterward, flipping into a turn, I heard a phone
ring and saw the guard in the loose gray sweatsuit
make his way to the back. I put on some speed and
had just reached the deepest part of the water when
the round blue-white eyes of the pool went dead, the
incongruous overhead chandeliers vanished, the fake
candles along the walls went black. The only light

remaining came from the two small glass squares in the swinging doors and from the upper stories of the neighboring skyscrapers, which glowed through the tinted glass of the sun lounge like lanterns in a thick brownish mist. I was surprised, then annoyed. Thinking it had been that kind of day, I swam over to the edge. A figure moved on the narrow strip of tiling that rimmed the pool and, believing it was the guard come to warn me to get out of the water, I asked, "Did a fuse blow?"

There was no answer. Though I automatically gripped the side of the pool and tensed to push back into the water, my alarm came too late. Something swept in an arc across the glitter of the apartment houses and connected with the side of my head. I fell back into the water, where I swallowed a mouthful before another blow struck my shoulder. I thrust myself away from the edge, gasping for breath. The dim figure moved again and with a kick, I plunged into the deepest part of the pool.

There was no light at all underwater, and my hands touched bottom, scraping my fingers. I surfaced, coughing on the water I had choked down, and saw someone rush out through the swinging doors. From the guard's room came a thunderous banging. When this failed to free the door, he began roaring into the telephone. Almost instantly, a porter and a repairman burst in. They wedged the doors open, played their flashlights all round, and released the guard, who came racing over the deck, all questions and apologies, as I started to haul myself from the pool.

"I'm fine. Some nut hit me. And ran out the door. I don't know—"

The lights snapped back on. I blinked and saw the guard turn pale.

"Don't move, don't move!" he exclaimed and began yelling for towels and the first aid kit.

I thought this was strange until I wiped the water out of my eyes and found my hand red with blood. Over my shoulder, I saw the perfect aquamarine of the pool disfigured with a dissolving red plume; dark spatters of the same marred the cream tiles. All this nastiness seemed to be coming from my head, which immediately began to sting, and from my aching shoulder, which sported a long, red welt.

There were cries for the manager, for the hotel doctor, and, on my part, for the person who had doused the lights and bashed my head. Rather ineffectual moves in that direction were made by the porter, now joined by two of his colleagues. Meanwhile, the guard poured antiseptic over my head and shoulders and loudly conveyed the regrets of the management, while disclaiming any responsibility for the "power outage," which, he theorized, would ultimately be traced to ConEd. I said that this was nonsense, that the hall lights had been on the whole time, and that I was going to my room.

Immediately I was assured that everything would be fine, that the doctor would arrive any minute, and that the scar(!) could be hidden with a new hairstyle. Before the babbling guard could convince me I was mortally injured but without, of course, grounds for a suit, I got up, grabbed a few towels to ward off the chill and stanch the persistently dripping blood, and headed for the door, my nervous entourage in pursuit. I was halfway to the elevator when a slender man in a suede jacket whipped a camera from his satchel and began snapping pictures. He managed three before a rhubarb broke out, with the lifeguard grabbing for the camera and a porter jumping between me and the lens. The photographer was up on all the tricks of the trade, however. Quick as well as opportunistic, he ducked to one side then took off for the stairs like a sprinter. Despite a lot of shouting, he made a clean getaway with the pictures, which were prominently displayed the next morning in *The Daily News*.

Of their kind, they were pretty good. I'd been given the dying-gangster treatment with some high-contrast touch-ups that turned the bloody smear on my forehead into a dark and sinister flood. With the doctor on one side and the guard reaching out dramatically for the offending camera, I was the focal point of a nice, splashy composition. The caption screamed "Laz Jinx III" and quoted Marylin Brook's surprise and shock. Very likely, I thought. That, at least, was Harry's reaction.

"I didn't think you read the News," I said.

"Jan picked it up. You know he loves anything supernatural. Imagine my joy."

"You should know better than to pay attention to news hype," I said, but I wasn't feeling too happy. There's a reason why great detectives aren't married. "No real damage done. You know how photos can be touched up."

"Like your explanations," Harry said. He was worried, and worry made him angry, and if I wasn't careful, we'd have a long-distance quarrel.

"Listen, I'm fine and I'll call you tonight. I've got to check the other papers and give the hotel some grief.'' I hung up before he could describe the grief I was giving him and took out my feelings on the embarrassed hotel emissaries, whom I dispatched for copies of the other city papers.

The news was all bad. *Daily Variety* had also run the story, adding some gossip about the high stakes involved in the Independence Mutual negotiations and the ongoing Brook litigation. But it was the good, gray *Times* that sealed my fate and sent my tasteful color-coordinated phone ringing off the hook. Some overachieving reporter had remembered me from another case; my cover was blown, and Valon's discreet little investigation went out the window in a tidy little story identifying me as the proprietor of a ''very exclusive private investigation and security service.''

Valon was not gratified by this endorsement of his good taste. ''I told you I saw no reason to go further into this matter'' were his opening words, and he refused to be mollified. ''I asked you to look into the case because I believed everything would be handled in a discreet and tactful manner. The Board of Directors is very displeased; I've been on the carpet already this morning.'' Valon's well-bred New England voice came as near a wail as I imagine it could get.

I apologized profusely but managed to hint broadly at my own personal peril and injury. ''It was totally unexpected. I should think this would convince the Board that there was something to my reservations. Brook, McNab, the caretaker, and now me, it's obvious that—''

''It's obvious to me, Ms. Peters, that you don't understand corporate policy as well as you claim.''

"Corporate politics, let's make that," I said. I wasn't feeling in the best temper myself.

"Either way, you're off the case. Entirely. A check will be in the mail this morning. And let me warn you against making any further inquiries in our name whatsoever."

"You're not talking about a measly million-dollar life policy anymore, you realize."

"What do you mean?"

"If I'm right, the whole *Lazarus Gambit* policy comes into question. For heavens' sake don't let them settle on that until—"

Valon cut me off. "I'll be lucky if I'm settling what you refer to as 'measly million-dollar policies.'" In a more conciliatory manner, he added, "I'm assured you weren't badly hurt—I'm glad of that."

"You'll see my claim," I said. "Independence Mutual carries my policy." I hung up before I could be goaded into telling Valon anything for free and relieved my feelings further by kicking the phone off the bedside table. Damn, damn, damn.

Then I got up, threw off my invalid pajamas—impressively spotted with blood—and pulled on a pair of slacks before deciding that today I would need all my war paint. I changed into a silk suit and heels and covered the missing snip of hair and the bandaged stitches with what the anxious hotel millinery shop had declared "the chicest little beret." Thus prepared, I had another cup of coffee, courtesy of the suddenly obliging room service, and tried to put aside embarrassment—and a newly returned concern for my finances.

Fact: I had not been hurt. Total damage, five stitches, some missing hair, a nasty bruise.

Fact: My assailant had arrived without a weapon—or had relied on using the pole kept hanging alongside the water. Either way, the attack had an improvisational feel and perhaps a feminine touch. In conjunction with the strategically placed photographer, it had been designed to surprise and embarrass rather than injure.

That suggested two interesting possibilities. First, that whoever attacked me was probably not McNab's assailant. Second, if that was correct, there was more than one person anxious for the termination of the Independence Mutual investigation, and each of the parties was acting alone.

I picked up the papers and began a more rational consideration of them. The photographer was identified as Lyle Nauchbor, and a little effort produced his number. I've done enough work in New York to have a few helpful friends. The second thing of interest was that while I had found Marylin Brook reticent and hard to contact, not one but two newspapers had found her willing to speculate on the jinx surrounding the *Lazarus* project and to express her deep regret that injury had now come to the insurance investigator employed by the company she was fighting in court. Tell me another.

An examination of the pool area last night and a talk with the guard this morning had convinced me that two people would have been needed: one to distract the lifeguard with a phone call, the other to kill the lights and lock the door to his office. The guard said he was sure his caller was a young woman. She had claimed to be from the linens department, but a check of the workers on duty revealed three older women, all with marked accents of one type or another. I had absorbed this, murmured something about a possible practical joke, and assured them that it would not be necessary to call the police. The spread in the papers had been an embarrassing surprise to the hotel as well as to me.

However, in addition to a number of stitches, a conspicuous bandage, and a fiscal loss, I had Nauchbor's name and number. After wasting some time trying to recall the precise tone of Marylin Brook's voice, I decided against an attempt at impersonation. If Nauchbor knew her well enough to venture out on a tip, he'd probably recognize her voice. I dialed and waited.

"Yeah?"

"Mr. Nauchbor? Marylin Brook's secretary. She thinks there may be another good picture possibility."

"Yeah?" Then suspicious "She didn't say any thing about that when she called this morning."

I smiled and put down the phone. I had Marylin Brook. If she had attacked me, why not Arthur McNab? And her late husband? This was a tempting line of thought but I found myself hesitant to carry it too far. Arthur McNab had nearly been killed and certainly there had been no photographers, no fanfare. My case was different. It had been a diversion aimed at getting me off the Independence Mutual investigation, and as such, it had succeeded—at least officially. I was no longer working for Independence Mutual, but there was nothing to say I couldn't take an interest on my own, especially when my personal reputation was at stake—and when the lowest figure mentioned was one million dollars.

Keeping that inspiring amount in mind, I found myself quite able to set out for a little talk with the other factor in the equation, Len Rossol.

ELEVEN

I CAUGHT UP WITH Rossol at a puce-colored, window-less fortress ornamented with an arched entry and a vintage marquee that winked New Biograph Studio. Inside was a long, spare foyer with a fluorescent-nourished plant and framed artwork from earlier Rossol productions. A receptionist buffed her nails at a steel console covered with phone wires like gray spaghetti, while a desiccated guard in a maroon uniform spun her a complicated yarn.

"Mr. Rossol will be tied up all morning, I'm afraid. If you'd care to leave your name."

"I need to see Mr. Rossol right away. I'm Anna Peters. I'm investigating the insurance claim on *The Lazarus Gambit* for Independence Mutual."

"But he's in the studio." Her reverent tone assured me that the great man was creating.

I took off my hat to display my impressive bandage. "Mr. Rossol will want to see me," I repeated. "There's been an accident that could conceivably complicate his insurance settlement."

"Oh, the settlement." She ran through a repertory of expressions, finally decided on resolute efficiency, and began pushing buttons at virtuoso speed. Dressing for success, I could see, had nothing on a few well-placed stitches and the threat of a big monetary loss.

I was announced in hushed and apologetic tones. The phone crackled a reply and she replaced the receiver, mightily impressed. "Mr. Rossol will be down right away."

"Thank you."

"If you'd just take a seat."

I thanked her again, very much on my best behavior, declined an offer of coffee, and was admiring a drawing done for the promotion of *Borodino* when Rossol swept out of the elevator.

"Anna, how good to see you. What happened? You weren't seriously hurt? Come on, you've got to tell me everything. We'll go upstairs."

In this shower of questions and concern, I was ushered to the elevator. As the doors rolled closed, his face lost its joviality and grew tight and strained. "I saw the papers," he said.

"I guess everyone did. It was nicely planned."

"What do you mean?"

"You're a pro, Len. How do you promote a picture? Publicity and timing. A clever stunt never hurt either, did it? This was the perfect combination: a little blood, a little sensation, even a quote from the grieving widow."

He cleared his throat. "Marylin's quite a gal."

"Yes."

"I didn't think she'd go that far."

I didn't commit myself, interested to see how far he'd take the idea.

"Our floor." He smiled his buccaneer's smile and held the door. "Hat suits you."

"Thanks."

"Yeah, Marylin's not been herself for a while."

"The shock of her husband's drowning?"

"From before that. Listen, Belinda's an all right

kid—a little mixed up, maybe—but she was no good for Henry. And that gave Marylin problems. You know how it is.''

"Were there serious problems between the Brooks? I thought the divorce was amicable.''

"Amicable, maybe. Tranquil, never. And he'd always driven her crazy about money. If he'd lived to be a hundred, she'd never have gotten their affairs untangled and her money out.''

We reached a corridor lined with offices, and Len stopped before one. "In here, unless you'd like to visit the studio—while I still have it.''

"I'd like the tour.''

"Fine. We had to renovate all this, of course. We'll start with makeup.'' He opened a door and gestured toward a row of barber chairs facing a long mirror. An assortment of wigs waited on forms. "Maxie's not in today, but she could make you a star.''

"A real talent.''

"You're so right.'' He opened one of the makeup kits filled with greasepaint and mascaras, then caught my eye in the mirror. "What's this visit really for? You may not know it, but the honchos from Independence Mutual were on the phone this morning assuring me you'd gone home.''

I should have expected it. Insurance companies are allergic to even a hint of bad publicity. "I'm overly conscientious,'' I said lightly. "I thought you'd like a personal account.''

"How kind. I'd had the feeling…'' He broke off and smiled. I could see the charm switch on, but instead of asking what had happened, he immediately led me to the stairs. "Down here for the wardrobe rooms. The old-time studios had their own clothes, their own dressmakers, tailors, everything. We couldn't afford that. Bought some, rented some, had a few made.''

On the next level, rows of black SS uniforms hung on racks next to brown shirts, some striped concentration camp pajamas, and a rack of murky print dresses. ''You could outfit a regiment,'' I said, surprised at their numbers.

''That's the wonderful thing about these places. It's all here. It's all real. Like a time capsule you can climb into.''

''I'd pick another era, thanks just the same.''

''Last time for moral clarity,'' he remarked. ''And the last time when expediency really excused.''

''Which attracts you?''

''That's the sort of question my shrink asks. Here are Kleinz's costumes. The last one's pretty good, don't you think?'' It was a linen summer suit in a very light beige. ''Designed to stand out against the uniforms.''

''The almost-good guy wears pale beige?''

''You don't care for him, do you?'' he asked, as if Kleinz had been real, which, I suppose, he had been.

''Not much.'' I pulled out one of the suits and was surprised at its size. ''I thought Brook was a bigger man.''

''Gift of the camera. It's interesting how many leading men have been undersized. Camera angle corrects most of the problems. Altheia was a bit tall for him but you wouldn't have known it.''

''He'd have been rather light, too.''

"Maybe one-thirty-five, one-forty. Still on the case?"

"Just my own curiosity. I find it disturbing that two people connected with the picture should have been injured since Brook drowned."

Rossol slid back the rack that held the actor's costumes and began to fiddle with a row of dresses. "See these? War-era cotton. We found a few bolts in a Seventh Avenue warehouse. Really adds to the authenticity."

I said nothing.

He pushed the hangers back with a snap. "What else, props? We don't have too many of our own. Special effects? You interested in electronic equipment? No? Then the stages. This way." We started down some narrow iron stairs. When we reached the bottom, he returned to the subject of the attacks. "I wouldn't take all this too seriously," he said in an avuncular manner. "It's easy to let a fright influence one's judgment. You said yourself—this way, first door—that it was probably a publicity stunt. Maybe an attempt to embarrass the company during litigation. You know lawyers."

"And McNab?"

"The caretaker? Unconnected. Just a coincidence."

"He nearly died, you know."

"That bad?"

"I went to see him."

Rossol's face grew a shade more serious. "Right through here." He unlocked a panel in the steel doors that stretched from floor to ceiling, and we stepped into the great cavern of the soundstage. High above the floor was a grid of catwalks and tracks, only half illuminated by scattered points of light; underfoot, electrical cables sprawled and coiled like snakes. There were a number of partitions erected on the floor and, in the center, three sides of a large roofless hall hung with Nazi regalia and furnished with wooden folding chairs. One end of this stage room was taken up by a dais with a podium flanked with chairs and backed by a huge red-and-black swastika.

"For the rally?"

"That's right. We haven't struck the set yet. There's actually quite a bit of interest in the documentary."

"Helped, no doubt, by the continuing interest in the *Lazarus* jinx."

"Not my doing, but I won't refuse a gift horse."

"Whose doing is what I'd like to know."

"Look, I told you, Marylin has had problems. You're not hurt. I wouldn't take it too seriously."

"The caretaker's only just gotten out of the hospital."

"I know that kind of town. 'Outsiders' get the blame for everything. What a bunch of bigots. That's how I researched *Gambit*—hanging around small towns. You'll see it was one of their own."

"You weren't there last Friday, were you?"

"Is that a serious question?"

"It's a serious business."

He hesitated. I think he was tempted to say he was in California but he was too clever for that. "I was in the city, as it turns out."

"You postponed your trip to the Coast?"

"Had to. Talks with some of the television people

interested in the documentary. As I said, we're just about in business with that.''

"I thought that was all up to the insurance company."

"Thanks to you, I think I'm in a stronger position this morning. They've been embarrassed—outside investigator revealed—believe me, I appreciate it. Independence Mutual's got to know they haven't any grounds to deny the claim. *Lazarus Gambit* cannot be completed as a big-budget thriller. Everyone's agreed. If I can recoup anything with the documentary, the company stands to benefit. It's in everyone's interest."

"Yet they've delayed settling."

"Careful of those cables. See the chairs? Old union hall stuff. Perfect. Independence Mutual has delayed settling, number one, because they're a bunch of bastards, and number two, because they thought they could panic me and I would settle for less than the face value of the policy. Wrong on both counts."

"So far."

"What do you mean?"

"You owe money on all this. Some of your notes are coming due. It's a matter of timing, isn't it?"

"Hence the documentary. A little time. That's all I need."

"Unfortunate you didn't think of a documentary to be cut along with the film."

"What would have been the point of that?" He stopped, one hand resting on his authentic union hall chairs.

"Oh, I don't know. It might have taken off some of the pressure to bring *Gambit* in on time. There was

a certain time pressure, wasn't there? Especially when
Brook began getting his attacks of temperament—or
whatever."

"Temperament," he said coldly.

"Try photic epilepsy."

If Rossol was surprised, he concealed it well.
"That's insurance company jargon. It's as rare as tits
with talent."

"You knew about his illness, though. Before."

Len gave me an unpleasant look. "You have gotten
around. All right, I did know. I didn't believe it."

"You should have. Berlin in flames delayed
you—how long? Ten days?"

"Henry Brook delayed us. Petty spite, little psychic
games. Henry couldn't stand to lose out. He was losing it. Getting a little too old to charm every broad
that came along. The real problem with Henry Brook
was that he couldn't face the fact that the only woman
who was going to stick by him was Marylin, the
Dragon Lady of Greenwich Village."

"Whatever he did before the Berlin scenes, he gave
them a good try. And he couldn't manage it, could
he? There were too many lights, too many special
effects, too much gadgetry."

"My fault, in other words," Rossol said angrily.
"I had a picture to bring in, lady. I had bills to pay.
I can't hold every actor's hand. Jesus Christ! They all
want their hands held. They all need special treatment. I'd rather work with horses. Yes, it was too bad
about Henry. Yes, if I'd known before the Berlin
stuff, I'd have doubled for him or used rear projection. Hell, I'd have done something different. Yes, it
got him down. Yes, and damn it, I'm paying for the

errors, too. You're right, I'm going to lose this studio. Ten years' work down the drain because a conceited, overage sex symbol can't be honest and face things the way they are.''

"So he died by 'misadventure'?"

"That's what they decided," Rossol said more easily. "Would you like to see how he should have died? As Dr. Kleinz, I mean. It would have been very dramatic. The rally set can conclude the documentary if Sir Michael can make a little time. We thought we might shoot some of his appearance as Hitler.''

"Hitler was on the London stage some time ago, wasn't he?''

"You have a good memory. But our Hitler's much more realistic, a drooling, blithering old idiot, which is what he'd have wound up as. He was a real druggie, you know.''

"I didn't know.''

"Morell, his physician, tested patent medicines on him. Really. The old quack made a fortune in the drug business and *der Führer* tested every one of them, usually in combination.'' Rossol drew me through a door to another set, much smaller and quite dark. "We would have used this for the awakening scene.'' When he switched on the light, I saw an old metal bedstead and some straight, Spanish-style chairs arranged before a window curtained in white gauze.

"We would have put in some low lights," he continued, "to get big shadows. Lots of brown, a real Goya light. They bring him in through that door—the old faithful in their brown shirts and SS gear—and put him on the bed.'' As Rossol smiled, the lights caught the abrupt planes of his face and glittered off his tinted glasses.

"Why all this in the studio? Why not on location?"

"I'll tell you a secret. I'd have preferred the old days with everything artificial, everything made to order. That's when the filmmaker had total control. All this location work—some of it's wonderful, no doubt, but one of the things I wanted to do was minimize that. I had to compromise on *Gambit* because the exotic locations were part of the book's appeal, but I wanted as much control as I possibly could, and with the new techniques and equipment available today you can do so much."

"Back to *Caligari?*"

"*The Cabinet of Dr. Caligari?* You know that? I love it. My ideal and all studio made, all fabricated. Very German. Of course the Germans don't write thrillers, that's British territory. The British are more realistic, less obsessive."

"Even in this story?"

"The obsession is my touch. That and the slant on the characterizations. I thought of one of Goya's *caprichos*—they've all become grotesque."

"Kleinz too?"

Rossol grew thoughtful. "Kleinz has become a grotesque of a different kind. He isn't deformed by ugliness like the old fascists. He's deformed by repentance. He is driven to expiate."

"With reason, I'd say."

"For him," Rossol said softly, "the only expiation is blood. Eye for an eye. He doesn't know it, but he is looking for destruction."

"How convenient it would be if all killers were so literal minded."

Rossol changed the subject. "I had to cut a lot of the book. The plots and counterplots, the Israelis' plans. Have you read the novel?"

"Not all of it."

"A labor. The Israelis and Agent Butterfly use Kleinz to locate Hitler. She has the usual feminine mixture of feelings." He made the adjective sound undesirable, as if he was not a man who really liked women.

"You're a bit cynical about your heroine, aren't you?"

"Altheia Karl has hidden shallows," he replied sourly, and I guessed that her prim self-sufficiency had offended him. "Anyway, they arrive at the rally. Kleinz obsessed with doing away with Hitler; Agent Butterfly trying to protect her lover; the other agents set to capture a really good bag. They meet here." Rossol waved his hand like a magician and stepped into the arena set. "Music, flags, crowds, tension. Shadows outside, a storm coming—crude, I admit, but surprisingly effective; the eye is rarely refined. We'd have started with a very long shot, low, then tracking in, in down the aisles to the podium. Cut to the scene from the rear entrance, Hitler's vantage point. In the back room, quiet. Then the door opens on the rally, the noise, the flags. Sir Michael would have been brilliant, the halting walk, the hypnotic eyes. He begins to speak, hesitantly at first, then furious, ranting. He's back in Berlin in spite of the sun and the palms, and he says they'll never surrender; he talks of victory, and the eastern front, *liebes-*

traum—it's all in his testament, we helped ourselves.
The delivery's the key, though. The guy's a wreck, a
shambles, mad. But the crowd is delirious; for them
it still works, the magic is still there; they're lost in
it. The camera moves in a long, curving loop, examining the faces of the crowd until we come to
Kleinz.''

Rossol was quite caught up in his narrative. I could
see why he was a great director. He had the flair and
the conviction to make people see things through his
eyes. Listening to him, I could imagine the crowd, the
tension, the obscene grouping on the platform, the
feeble and repulsive insanity of the director who had
returned almost literally from the dead.

''Kleinz begins to work his way to the front,'' Rossol said. ''No one notices him, everyone is rapt. Now,
we begin cutting back to the Israelis, who are outside
the building, getting set to haul themselves up on the
roof and in through a skylight. Butterfly is trying to
persuade them to spare Kleinz or to kill him in the
raid instead of taking him prisoner. They refuse.
They're convinced it's all in their control, in their
power. They all make the same mistake,'' Rossol
said, his face glistening under the hot lights, ''they
all think they can control events.''

I nodded and he moved to the dais before continuing. ''Back to Kleinz. He's near the platform—we'd
have had to rehearse this very carefully so that the
distances would be right. He says, 'It was my work.
You are my fault. You should have died in Berlin,'
and raises his old service pistol.''

With a sense of deep unease, I saw Rossol reach

behind the podium and produce a very authentic-looking revolver.

"The goons are on him in a minute. He gets a shot off," Rossol said, pivoting to face the dais, "but it misses Hitler. Up on the roof, the Israeli agents hear the commotion and move. There's panic in the hall. Butterfly gets to a window, sees Kleinz attacked, and begins picking off the distinguished guests on the platform. Total chaos. Now, here's where Sir Michael comes into his own. This is why I got him, and the time, the effort, to persuade the old fool, you wouldn't believe. Hitler's been left alone, an idiot lost in the crowd. Without the audience's attention, he switches off. Kleinz is being worked over by the goons, the honored guests are getting shot by Butterfly, the rest are running and screaming. Hitler sees the pistol Kleinz has dropped." Rossol turned the prop weapon in his hand as if illustrating what he wanted from the actor. "The last thing he remembers was his plan to use just such a weapon in the Berlin bunker. There's this quite incredible monologue while he's standing there with the gun, chaos all around him. Then the camera spots an agent who sees him and begins fighting his way forward, through the mob; the agent almost reaches him, he's almost there, when Hitler, mistaking the noise and shots for the arrival of the Red Army in the bunker, puts the gun in his mouth and pulls the trigger."

Rossol stopped his account with the gun raised beside his face, swallowed, and said nothing more, leaving me to read the sequence of events in the subtle shift of his expressions.

"And Kleinz?" I asked finally.

Rossol lowered the gun but did not lay it aside. "Half dead. Butterfly gets to him, drags him outside in the confusion; he dies in her arms, convinced he's done something against the evil he assisted. At the end, Butterfly arranges to have him decently buried, though how Altheia would have managed that scene I can't imagine." He shrugged. "Still, it would have been a good flick."

"Yes, I'm sorry."

"Well, a film is always a gamble," he said philosophically.

"The reason studios carry insurance?"

"Precisely." His eyes grew colder with remembrance. "And now you're off the case, maybe I'll collect my money."

"Maybe it will come in time," I replied. I know how to be unpleasant too.

"They've no choice," Rossol said, fiddling idly with the pistol.

"Unless they choose to gamble."

"Gamble on what, Anna?"

"You're the master of fiction and suspense. You know what would bail them out. If they prove suicide, Marylin loses, but you win. But suppose they prove murder—with intent to defraud?"

"Then Marylin wins, and I lose. Very neat. You should consider pictures. But they'll never prove I killed the star of my own picture and jeopardized my career and my studio, not to mention my freedom. I like your style, but it won't play in Peoria."

"It plays rather better in upstate New York," I said.

Now he laughed easily, as if relieved at the trifling

quality of my suspicion. "The trouble with Arthur? Now that might make a title."

"It might make something else, along with your money troubles and your dislike for Henry Brook."

"Listen, in this business, bastards are a dime a dozen. An occupational hazard."

I found it curious in all this that he never defended himself in the obvious way with the fact that Brook had drowned.

"Now," he continued, "you're looking for a man—or a woman." He studied the revolver, then looked up quickly, his eyes intense, as if there had been a sudden concentration of energy. "Someone ruthless but farsighted. Calculating." He gave a half-smile. "Someone who would remember this weapon." He held it up for my inspection.

"Careful with that."

"You're not keen on firearms? I'm a little disappointed. I'm not sure I like the feminine touch in detection. But you're right to be cautious. There are a number of stories of theatrical tragedies—of guns loaded with the wrong ammunition. That sort of thing. It's more likely to happen on stage with the fake knives, but it's not implausible around a movie studio, is it?"

"The more reason for care." My mouth was beginning to feel dry.

"You're not as cool as you seem," Rossol said accurately. "I'm considered a great ham, but I'm good at detecting fake emotion. It's one of my directorial strengths." He stepped closer to me, effectively blocking the exit from the soundstage. "The other is my enthusiasm, my ability to convince even the mediocre performers that great things are possible, that the scene is doable, that all the fakery of the set can be made real. I often act out every detail of a scene. With props.'' He looked at me slyly. ''Now, this gun is a prop, and I'm doing the climactic scene of *The Lazarus Gambit* for you.''

I edged back and began to look for a means of distracting him, but Rossol had picked his spot well. There was nothing within reach, and worst of all, I was still uncertain of his true intentions. Ham actor or not, he was good enough to scare me.

''Don't go away,'' he said, as I reached the first row of seats. ''It doesn't matter when I fire. My habits are well known. I throw myself into every scene. I was demonstrating, I got carried away and...'' He stopped. ''Do you believe me? You look doubtful. I've always found doubt the most painful of emotions. Uncertainty is real torture in some situations, wouldn't you agree?'' He raised the revolver and, keeping it trained on me, shifted his ground so that he was in the proper position for Dr. Kleinz's last stand. ''This is a test of your theory, so in a sense, you'll win either way.'' He brought his other hand up to the gun to steady his aim, and I tried to realize that I was going to be shot, perhaps killed. I didn't believe it. It was too bizarre. I was on a studio set, surrounded by swastikas and wooden folding chairs. There were catwalks laden with electrical gear and floodlights burning overhead. It would not happen. It would. I felt a sudden dangerous acquiescence, then forced myself to reach back to the chairs. I would turn around and gamble that he wouldn't dare shoot me in the back, but I couldn't move. I will turn around, I told myself, and walk out, I will—

Rossol came a step nearer. "Kleinz sees Hitler. He raises the pistol. 'You should have died in Berlin,' he says and—"

I dived onto the floor, overturning the nearest chairs, then throwing myself into the next row. The gun discharged once, then again, and as I struggled to my feet, ready to run for my life, Rossol broke into a loud laugh and fired again and again, the last time directly at his own forehead. I disentangled myself from the chairs, ripping my good silk suit in the process.

"There you have it," he announced, "a little demonstration of the difference between theater and life. In life you'd be dead. I'd be up for—manslaughter, maybe? I've a terrific lawyer. With lots of good testimonials, I might even get off."

I wanted to hit him. I wanted to scream a lot of dirty, vulgar things and throw something that would break. Instead, I said, "Who loaded the gun? Wouldn't that be the question?"

"But you wouldn't be around to ask. Aren't you glad this was just improvised? I can see you're shaking under that assumed sangfroid. I'm a connoisseur of good acting, and you're just an amateur."

He was a hateful, manipulative man, and I could feel my professional control begin to fray. Doubtless, I would have said something disastrous if a man hadn't yelled, "Mr Rossol! Mr. Rossol!" and banged the studio door open.

"The discoverers of your unhappy end now arrive

to find me in grief-stricken shock,'' he said archly, then called, "over here!"

A man in work clothes appeared at the back of the set. "I heard shots."

"Just blanks." Rossol held up the pistol. "I was demonstrating how we proposed to end *The Lazarus Gambit* for one of the insurance representatives. She was very impressed."

"Sorry to disturb you, Mr. Rossol. We were worried. You know the neighborhood."

"It's all right. You can show Ms. Peters back to the front desk. I've got to run." He looked at his watch. "Late already. Well, Anna, since you're going to D.C., this is goodbye." He took my damp hand and smiled at this confirmation of my fear. Len Rossol liked to be in control; he enjoyed showing who was boss. "Joe will take you back. And Joe, you might lock this in the prop department. It should never have been left out. The neighborhood, as you say."

"Oh, sure, Mr. Rossol. I thought it had been accounted for."

"We all make mistakes," he said smoothly, "even clever lady investigators." Then he smiled and waved goodbye as I was led off in total defeat.

Or almost total defeat. At the receptionist's desk, I forced myself to demand, in the huffiest manner possible, some stills of Belinda and a picture of Marylin Brook. Belinda was easy; there was a press packet on the desk. Marylin was a tougher order, and I feared Rossol might show up to check on my departure. Fortunately, he was overconfident. The receptionist located a picture of Mrs. Brook with her husband at the contract signing, and although she hesitated and thought she might "call and see if it's okay," my theatrical talents proved good enough to impress her if not her boss.

"Len said I was to have everything I needed," I insisted. "It's for the insurance company."

"Oh, well, I guess then it's all right."

"Yes," I said, taking the pictures and smoothing my torn suit. "He owes me."

TWELVE

I RODE BACK FROM the studio in a cab of dubious provenance, angry at the driver for his murderous chances, angry at Rossol for much the same reason, and most angry at myself for general stupidity. I had broken elementary rules and nearly paid for my carelessness, and as usual when there was no one else to blame, I was furious. My temper was not improved by the hotel manager who noticed my suit and bustled over, fearing the worst, nor by the first three porters who looked at the stills and shook their heads blankly.

"Who was on yesterday, late afternoon, early evening?"

There was a discussion about this. I learned that Jimmy and Hernandez had been on duty but that they would not be in until around three. More consultations discovered a doorman who had worked an extra shift for a friend, and I found him in the garage, deep in gossip with the cashier. He was elderly, straightbacked, and impressive in his braid-trimmed uniform, but his dark eyes were shadowed blue about the iris by approaching cataracts. I could not be optimistic.

"Was either of these women here yesterday?"

He took the photographs to study, sniffed, and raised his eyebrows before pointing to Belinda. "She has been here. Once, twice."

"Recently?"

"I got a cab for her."

"Yesterday? Last evening?"

"About seven she came in. With an older woman in a head scarf. One of those lace things."

"This woman, do you think?" I indicated Marylin.

"She is the right age. How tall?"

"A bit shorter than I am."

He glanced at my shoes to check the height of my heels. "It could have been, but her face has not stayed with me. This young woman," pointing to Belinda, "is easy to remember. Very thin, very pale, very nervous."

"That's her. Thank you."

"Thank you, ma'am." The bill disappeared as smoothly as a fish into water. I took the elevator to my room, where I was changing my clothes and gloomily wondering if I could salvage my professional honor with a visit to Mrs. Brook and Belinda, when the phone rang. It was Arthur McNab.

"Mr. McNab. How are you?"

"Much better, thank you. I've remembered something. It's just a little thing but you'd said—"

"Yes, of course." I sat down on the edge of the bed and reached for my notebook. "Go ahead."

"You had asked if anything had been lost by the film company, if anything had gone missing."

"That's right."

"It was just last night I remembered that the day after the company left, one of the electricians called me. They were short some piece of equipment after the party."

"Were you able to help him?"

"No, I wasn't. Jim and I, we only took down the

wooden frames and the light stanchions. All the wiring was to be shifted later. I explained that.''

"What did he say?"

"They were still short one 'flasher' is what he called it. It's a device that makes signs and lights blink.''

A host of possibilities took shape. "Good Lord!" I exclaimed.

"What?"

"Mr. McNab, this could be very important. Did they ever find it?''

"Not as far as I know. In fact, I'm sure they didn't because when we were out in the car last night, I saw it in use.''

In his prolix and roundabout way, McNab began filling me in, but I cut him off. "You know where it is?''

"Well, I'm pretty sure, as I was going to say—"

"Hold on. I'll be up to the village as soon as I can, Mr. McNab. It's three? I'll see you by five, five-fifteen.''

"Do you want me to try to get it?"

"No, no, when I come up.''

"Well, all right, but if it's a bother for you, I could—"

"Bother? Mr. McNab, you've made my day.''

And, I thought, as I set down the phone, fixed someone else but good. I jumped up, kicked off my city heels, and grabbed my slacks. Stopped, told myself sensibly that it was a long shot, that it was never going to be neat, that there were loose ends—then said, "To hell with you, Len Rossol," and raced down to the garage.

Traffic was bad that day, and it was closer to six than five when I arrived at the McNabs' cottage, a Victorian stucco with a peaked roof, lots of dark woodwork, and a Grimm's fairy-tale air relieved by a bed of pansies occupying the only sunny patch on the lawn. As I approached the steps, there was a great deal of barking, and I was pleased to recognize Hector's deep voice behind the door; I would have to warn the McNabs to keep him close by.

"Ah, it's Miss Peters. Arthur! It's Miss Peters."

"I'm afraid I'm going to disturb you again, Mrs. McNab."

"Come in, come in. Arthur's that pleased to be of help."

We shook hands all round, and I was pressed to sit down to supper, while the dogs ran back and forth in excitement, their nails clicking on the bare, polished boards.

"Out with this lot, now," Mrs. McNab said. "I'll not have dogs at the table."

There was a general shooing and ordering before the rear door slammed. "Do they stay around the house?" I asked.

"There's a run at the back."

"Good. Until this is over, I'd advise you to keep Hector, at least, around the house. If you like, I can arrange some other protection."

The McNabs' pleasant, animated faces turned solemn. "It's that serious? This thing Arthur remembers?"

"It could be. We're talking about forty million dollars potentially."

Mrs. McNab was surprised but not easily rattled

where hospitality was concerned. "You'll have potatoes?" she asked as she reached for my plate.

"Yes, please."

She ladled the stew over them and added carrots. "Enough money to tempt some," she observed judiciously.

"That would be from the movie policy?" Mr. McNab asked.

"That's right. Henry Brook was insured. That's one policy. Then the production itself was insured."

"How could one little piece of equipment be so important?"

"It might show us how Brook came to drown. Might. I can't be sure yet, so I'd rather not go into the matter. The biggest thing in favor of the idea is the attack on you. And the fact that your workshop had been rifled. Was anything missing there, incidentally?"

"Not so much as a box of nails."

"Someone thought you had it. Who from the village worked on the party or did work for the film company?"

"Well," said McNab, "there was myself. I had the most contact with them, because I was asked to oblige once in a while with runs to Poughkeepsie. For the party—who was in to help that night, Kit?"

"They got the caterers in from the village. The Santellis, father, son, two girls. And Meg Potter and I helped serving the drinks and so forth.

"Was there a bar man?"

"Bar woman. The Carroll girl was home from college."

"What about outside? The day I first came here,

you mentioned something about setting up decorations.''

"That was the film crew—and me. I didn't like to intrude, but I felt responsible with the Delfs away. If there had been any damage, it would have come back to me, you know.''

"Perhaps you'd better describe these decorations.''

"Oh,'' Mrs. McNab said with a laugh, "if you'd seen them. Such a carry-on.''

"There were balloons and streamers in the summerhouse,'' her husband said. "Then they had bunting—that was pinned up over the doors. I was a bit worried for the woodwork. And a banner outside with all the cast's and crew's names on it. The lights were the main thing, though. They ran stanchions down the jetty and along the whole dock area.''

I took a last mouthful of stew and pushed my plate aside so that I had room for my notebook. "The jetty runs like this, as I remember.'' I did remember, having made a sketch the day I'd gone to see it.

"That's right. Well, here were the stanchions, far as I can recall. One here, two at each end, and the rest all along; about six feet apart they were.''

"We can double-check from the marks of the nails.''

"Oh, right you are.''

"Now, these were erected by the set carpenters?''

"Yes. I was around, held a board now and again but no heavy work.''

"And the set electricians strung the wires?''

"That's right. Mr. Rossol was there too. Like I told you before, he could turn his hand to anything. They ran the cables, put up the lights. Very fussy he was about the sizes of the bulbs. They had to be just right. Like little candles, they were, but bright.''

I could imagine. There was only one thing—''Did these flicker?''

''The bulbs? Oh, no, all the best stock.''

''Then this thing they were missing, the 'flasher,' what was it for, do you think?''

''I don't really know. Probably, it wasn't for the decorations at all, see, they probably just left it lying around. Like I told you, it was a little thing, not really all that important.'' He said this regretfully, as if sorry to have had me waste my time.

I shook my head. ''Leave that for a minute. Was there anyone else from the village?''

''Just the fellow I think pinched it—Billy Davies. His dad owns the local bar. You'll not have seen it, the way you come in. The Pine Grove. Well, Billy, who's a friend of the younger Santelli boy, got himself delegated for cleanup, trucking empties around, dumping cans afterwards. He's a big, strong kid and always alert for the main chance.''

''Not the best sort of reputation,'' Mrs. McNab put in, prompting her husband to say, ''That was all ancient history. He's not a bad lad, but the sort who would pick up something handy if it didn't seem to have an owner,'' which I thought was a nice distinction.

''And why,'' I asked, ''would this flasher thing be useful to him?''

''Billy's good with anything electrical. After the other night—but you'd better see for yourself. We'll take a run down after dinner.''

So I was left in suspense, and, like a good storyteller, McNab switched to other topics until after supper when we got into the wagon and left the estate. I asked no questions, realizing that his sense of drama would be offended by untimely prying. As compensation, he offered a vast amount of interesting, if largely irrelevant information about Billy Davies, his family, and their niche in the village's complicated society. In cities, ignorance of one's neighbors can count as bliss; in the country, every man is a Balzac, and quiet monotony is relieved by gossip, genealogy, and speculative psychology. McNab was particularly good on the middle term of the triad. I received an account of three generations of Davies, who seemed to alternate between the liquor trade and petty mischief, and of their comedown from the glory days of Prohibition.

"There on the left," McNab said as we rounded a sloping, wooded curve, but no directions were needed. Not only was the little roadside tavern the only spot of neon for miles around, but both the letters and its trademark Christmas tree silhouette were flashing at an eye-blinding rate.

McNab pulled into the gravel parking lot and looked at me.

"How long's the sign been up?"

"The sign's been up for years, but until last night I never saw it flash."

"Had you seen it before you were hurt?"

"I was down here just before the party and it was plain then. It's since that piece of equipment went missing that The Pine Grove's got the flickering lights, and it's not something Billy bought either."

"How can you be sure?"

"Because before I called you, I asked the electrician, thinking he might have done the work. He not only didn't do it, but he tells me it's illegal to sell those flasher things now."

"Mr. McNab, I'm impressed." I looked at the sign, which was switching the letters off and on at a rate too fast for comfort. Attached to a double row of lights along the jetty, the device could have set up a pulsating flicker sufficient to precipitate an epileptic seizure. Getting Brook to the end of the dock would have been the only requirement. "But you're sure the lights at the party didn't flash."

"Not like that, they didn't. At least," he added more cautiously, "not that I saw."

"You've hit the key to it. Let's see if we can talk to Billy Davies."

"Could I make a suggestion?"

"Sure."

"Let me talk to Billy. You being a stranger..." He let the sentence die tactfully.

"Of course, but I need that flasher. If necessary I'll pay him for a proper blinking sign."

"I don't think that's required. He shouldn't have picked the thing up to start with."

"True, but for what's at stake, I'm not going to quibble. Don't hesitate to buy the whole damn thing."

McNab made a reluctant calculation of the costs before he got out of the wagon and led the way into The Pine Grove, a dimly lit tavern with a few tables, a mirror-backed bar, a jukebox, and, as a concession to modern tastes, a pair of video games beeping and whining in one corner.

"Well, Arthur," said the bartender, "you're up and

around and squiring younger women. I don't think Kit will excuse that along with the lump on your head.''

It was evident that everyone knew everyone else there, for the customers along the bar joined in with observations on this theme, and Arthur took their good-natured joshing without offense. ''Mike, this is Miss Peters,'' he said finally. ''From the insurance company.''

''Are you taking that dent on your head seriously?'' someone asked. Arthur received a drink in honor of his recovery; his injury was recounted twice—and corrected by the victim himself—and a good deal of subtle but persistent curiosity about my personality and business was fielded. I left all this to McNab, who hinted in a dozen interesting directions without revealing anything of substance.

Once we had drunk the ritual whiskey and the loafers had returned to the video games, the fortunes of the Mets, and the price of hay, Arthur leaned over to inquire if Billy was around.

''A little job, maybe?'' asked his dad.

''Might be a little profit in it,'' Arthur said.

''He's over at the garage tonight, helping Nicky out. Trouble with your car?'' he asked me.

''Just a little business talk, Mike,'' Arthur said. ''See you. Stay out of trouble, boys.''

I could hear the buzz as we walked to the door.

''Set them up for the evening, that will,'' Arthur said when we were outside. ''The excitement that film brought to town you'd hardly believe.''

The garage was a multipurpose outfit with gas pumps in the front, a display of bread, oranges, and soap powders in the window, and the steady drone of a motorcycle issuing from a lighted space in the back. "He's there, all right," said Arthur. "And his dad'll have called him," he added, for we had not even switched off the motor before a sturdy youth with blond hair shaved up the sides and a red freckled face came around the corner, wiping his greasy hands on an old towel. "'Lo, Arthur."

"Evening, Billy."

"Dad said you were coming by. Job up at the Delfs'?" He looked at me curiously as he spoke.

"This is Miss Peters," Arthur said and we shook hands. "She's an investigator with the film company."

Billy looked surprised and perhaps the least little bit unhappy. "Pleased to meet you."

"How are you?"

Arthur gave me a look as a reminder that he was to handle this errand.

"You remember, Billy, the party the film people threw?"

"It's you've been hit on the head, not me."

"It seems," Arthur continued, unperturbed, "that a piece of their electrical apparatus went missing."

"Don't look at me," Billy said too quickly. "I had nothing to do with the wiring—nor with them two bottles of French champagne that were taken, either."

"The help were entitled to some champagne," Arthur said smoothly, "but professional equipment's something else, and as caretaker, I get the comeback on it."

"Well, you best check with some of the others," Billy said.

"No one else there knows a thing about electrical

equipment, and the caterers went home early. It was the cleanup crew that had the opportunity. As a usual thing, no one would have bothered probably but there's that big suit on about the picture. It's been in all the papers, and now everything's got to be accounted for—even one little thing that makes a sign flash."

"Oh, come on!" Bill exclaimed. "You can ask around. I bought that flasher for the bar in Poughkeepsie."

"Did you? They're not made like that any more—illegal, so Tom tells me in the village. And you'll not tell me Tom Nolan doesn't know his stuff."

There was a certain amount of debate on this and so many protestations of innocence that I began to fear this fish would escape.

"It was no crime to pick it up," McNab allowed now, "seeing how lazy and careless they were with their equipment."

Billy agreed to this face-saving assessment with an uneasy glance at me. Although not the quickest of minds, he knew the flasher was outside Arthur's usual concerns.

"Now, I've said I'd see that the device was given back," Arthur concluded, ignoring all disclaimers, "and because the company's so pleased it was found, being they're not exactly made this same way anymore, Miss Peters here has kindly agreed to pay for any trouble connecting and disconnecting The Pine Grove sign."

Billy looked at me.

"That would be the arrangement," I said.

"How much? That's if I agree to do it."

"Well, now, what's electrician's rates?" Arthur asked. "Near twenty an hour?"

"Try twenty-five. And this is overtime."

"Still, fifty ought to do it," Arthur said. "I'd say that's a good deal, and there'd be no comeback."

Billy looked stubborn. "We're just talking," he said. "I'm not agreeing, but I think one hundred."

I nodded to Arthur. "But now. Tonight," I said.

"There'll be notice," Arthur warned.

"What time does The Pine Grove close?"

"Before midnight," Billy said, "except on weekends. Probably close up around eleven-thirty tonight."

This time was agreed on, and Arthur insisted on accompanying me back to The Pine Grove after hours. We found Billy's motorcycle in front, the neon sign out, and a ladder resting against the side of the building. Billy's silhouette appeared around the roof dormer. "That you, Arthur?"

"Right."

"Switch on the light, would you? I want to be sure it's properly connected."

Arthur felt around inside the door, then the pine tree and its Pine Grove sign ran pink and green.

"Okay. You can put it out."

There was a scramble on the roof as Billy descended with a square object about half the size of a cigar box and slightly thicker. Sandwiched between two plain metal plates were connections, points, and, as Billy pointed out, a set of rotating cams. "Cuts the current off and on. This one isn't quite right for a sign, anyway. Too fast a flicker. Hurts your eyes after a while.''

"I wonder what they used it for. Do you know?''

Billy was tempted by this appeal to his superior knowledge but still cautious. He shrugged.

"It's not the sort of thing they'd just leave lying around,'' I said thoughtfully. "I wonder if it wasn't part of the circuits for the party. Where did you find it?''

"On the ground. Someone had thrown it away.''

"Really? Would you swear to that?''

Billy looked uncomfortable. "What is this anyway? This is a crappy old thing that's not even made anymore. You heard Arthur.''

"It's not of any importance,'' I agreed, "but I like to be accurate. It's no problem for you either way, but I'm guessing you found this on one of the light supports, recognized its usefulness, and figured no one would miss it.''

"I don't know,'' he said, but his eyes were crafty. "That would be overtime rates.''

I had come prepared. "Let's sit in the wagon,'' I said, taking out my portable tape recorder. "This interview is premium rates. One hundred the half hour. Begin with your arrival at the party.''

Arthur shook his head in disapproval, but Billy proved a very interesting witness on two counts. First, he had indeed disconnected the flasher device from the jetty end of the party light circuit, and second, he had observed the lights flickering on several occasions during the evening.

Arthur disputed this instantly.

"Wait a minute," I said. "Where were you, Billy?"

"Outside on the hill. Me and Junior Santelli, we were lugging the cases of empties around, then we sat outside, had a few joints. I thought something was wrong with the circuit. Flicker, flicker, flicker."

"How long?"

"A minute or two."

"Where were you?" I asked Arthur.

"Most of the time I was in the main building keeping out unauthorized visitors. Some of them thought they should be allowed to traipse through the house. But I was down in the summerhouse, too, and the lights were fine. If they had been flickering on and off, someone would have noticed. It was never mentioned."

There was something in this, but my idea about the ultimate purpose of the device made me persist. "Exactly where were you on the hill, Billy?"

"There's this stone wall at the foot of the garden. We were sitting next to that."

"And what could you see?"

"I told you—the lights, the summerhouse, the lake."

"All the lights?"

"Well, the jetty lights. The near end of the dock would be behind the roof of the summerhouse."

"You were in the main building, Mr. McNab, or in the summerhouse proper?"

"The main house. And you can't see the jetty from there, that's true."

"And when you were in the summerhouse, it's the lights on the dock you'd be apt to notice."

"Yes, I suppose so."

I switched off the recorder, paid Billy, and put the tape in my case. "You've been a big help," I told him, "but I think Mr. McNab and I had better have a last look at the summerhouse."

Although Arthur was surprised and must have been curious, he asked no questions until he walked up to the top of the hill by the Delfs' garden, the flashlight we'd used to simulate the jetty lights in his hand. "A lot of fuss over this," he remarked.

"Essential, I'm afraid." I had no doubts now. Even the timing in Billy's testimony fit.

"Why were you so keen to get that flasher back? And why all this with the lights?"

The device lay in my hand like a fat sandwich. "This, Mr. McNab, is what killed Henry Brook."

"But how?" he asked, astonished.

"How is simple. What I've got to settle is who."

THIRTEEN

I WAS UP WITH the dawn, when the cattle pastured next to the motel got restless and entered the city along with the rush-hour mob. The Brook brownstone came into view well before nine, and, figuring they owed me a cup of coffee, I leaned on the bell until Mrs. Brook appeared, swaddled in an old bathrobe. Her face was gray without its usual makeup, but her charming disposition was already in place.

"Marylin," I said with feigned delight, "I happened to be in the neighborhood and thought I'd catch you now for sure."

She slammed the door, but I pressed the bell until it opened again—as far as the chain would allow. "I'll call the police."

"Fine. It'll save me the effort. Call your lawyer as well. Personal injury suits are bringing in quite a bit of coin these days and I'm planning to pursue the matter of the other night."

She didn't answer immediately, but I heard the chain rattle. She swung open the door and stepped aside, glancing at her watch as she did so. "Hell of a time to come visiting."

"This is a business call."

"Some business. Well, what have you got to say?"

"Is Belinda home? This concerns her too."

"She's getting ready for a shooting," Marylin said, turning to walk through an arched doorway to the dining room. Glasses for juice were set out on the table along with coffee cups, an oozing stick of margarine, and a stack of newspapers. As with the rest of the establishment, the room was a mixture of quality and squalor. There were crumbs underfoot, stains on the table, and bits and pieces of Belinda's wardrobe draped about the chairs. "Coffee?" Marylin asked. The cup was the best bone china and the none-too-clean glass beside it was cut crystal.

"Please."

"You're here early."

"I just came in from upstate."

She stopped pouring, looked at me sharply to see if I was telling the truth, then set down the pot. "Milk?"

"A little."

She pushed the cup toward me, ran her hand through her thick, untidy hair and adjusted her large tinted glasses. "I didn't know you knew the Delfs. They're old friends of ours, especially dear Celia, who's a charming person. I don't believe you can have met her."

"A pleasure I've missed." I hadn't seen Marylin Brook in her society mode before, either, but now I got the full treatment.

"We saw them here mostly. We were both on the board for the opera. The Met, of course, and I saw her at the Modern as well. She's one of the trustees. But we really got to know them one winter in Palm Beach. Henry was advised to take a complete rest, to get away from the film crowd. They're very stimulating, as all creative people are, but they're too aware of money; it's always deals, packages, and percentages. Now with people like the Jahred Delfs, there's none of that.'' She pursed her lips regretfully and added some coffee to her cup. ''I won't offer you breakfast,'' she added. ''Belinda and I are always dieting.''

''I'd have thought Belinda needed all the food she could eat.''

''You cannot be too thin in her business. It's impossible. Some models just wreck themselves—binges, vomiting, quite unhealthy. Fortunately, Belinda was meant to be thin. I only have to watch she doesn't indulge,'' Marylin said, showing a set of teeth like a piranha's. ''You probably think I'm hard, but she'd tell you—she'd have had no career without me. I shaped the look and now it's all over New York. The Continent is next, I think, but we'll have to change her a bit for that. They have an image of American girls as very wholesome, fresh, unsophisticated: beef on the hoof.'' She squinched her mouth at the competition.

''So you're leaving?''

''Oh, not for a while. Not for a while. Although I expect the case will be settled eventually.'' She gave me an arch, triumphant look. ''That business about Henry's medical form is not going to do it.''

''No?''

''His handicap had nothing to do with his death. Nothing at all. It was a freak accident and Independence Mutual is going to pay. Though why you should care, I don't know. Aren't you off the case?''

''More or less.''

''The papers,'' she said, patting one of the piles as if looking for the right one.

"There was apparently some distress at the home office," I conceded.

"You must admit, Anna, that your investigations were conducted in a somewhat spectacular fashion. All right for some cases, I'm sure, but with people as well known as Henry Brook or the Delfs, you cannot expect to get away with such stunts. Image," she said, giving me a savvy and calculating appraisal, "is the name of the game. That's turned out to be my talent." She nodded complacently and took a sip of coffee.

"Connections help, I'm sure," I replied, hinting at her friend the photographer, but Marylin was on her favorite topic.

"Part of the art. One of the things I've been able to do for Belinda—" There were footsteps on the stairs and she glanced up quickly. "'Bye, dear," she called.

"Belinda ought to stay," I said, "I'd canool the session if I were you, Belinda."

"Oh, it's Anna. We thought you were gone." Unlike Marylin, Belinda seemed vastly amused; she was bright-eyed and dressed in a very chic version of a painter's overalls in white linen.

"Belinda does not need any suggestions. Hurry up. You'll be late," Marylin said, consulting the large gold watch on her wrist. "Have you called a cab?"

"No, and now that Anna's here, I'll just wait." She turned to me. "You have a car, don't you?"

"Yes."

"Well, she can drop me. What have you been up to?" she asked as she rummaged through a variety of boxes and bags in the adjacent pantry. "This is it? One stale bagel?"

"Ounces, dear, ounces."

"Merde." Belinda began nibbling on the dry bagel. "We thought you'd left the city."

"I've been up visiting Arthur McNab."

Our last discussion of Arthur's injury had produced near hysteria. This morning, she never turned a hair. "How's he doing?"

"He's fortunate to be alive. He's going to be all right."

"Belinda told me about it," Mrs. Brook put in now. "I phoned Celia. Everyone was just devastated. Do hurry up, Belinda."

"I got rather a crack myself the other night." I pulled off my beret. "Five stitches."

"They've cut your hair!" Belinda exclaimed, suitably impressed. "But you were never in any danger, were you? The papers said—"

"My lawyers will decide that."

Belinda sat up straight and dropped the pose of careless innocence. "Your lawyers?"

"Yes," I said. We'd reached familiar territory: a confrontation between knowledge and money. But money I could get elsewhere. From Mrs. Brook and Belinda, I hoped for information and a lever to enlist Marylin's still powerful influence. "I intend to sue you—one or both, depending on what seems the better deal. Assault and battery, pain and suffering, defamation of professional character…my lawyers are creative."

"Get out," Marylin roared. "I knew I should never have let you in. I won't have this."

"I don't think you have any choice."

While she delivered a few select phrases, I fished

around in my case for the publicity stills. "Would it surprise you that the doorman at my hotel recognized both of you?"

I laid the pictures out on the table, and Marylin quieted down. "Such industry," she sneered, "and all of it so irrelevant."

"Even the fact that Belinda was identified as arriving shortly before I was injured?"

"Belinda? Look at her. She's barely one hundred pounds."

"The rescue pole at the pool doesn't weigh more than two or three, but let that go. I have no doubt that other hotel staff would recognize you and that the pool attendant would know your voice or, more likely, Belinda's."

"Belinda has been on half a dozen covers in the last year. Lots of people would think they knew her. And the hotel—I think we've been in every good hotel in the city. Meetings, interviews, you understand," she said, without quite managing to recapture the airy complacency she'd shown earlier. Belinda said nothing, but she'd stopped picking at her breakfast.

"Only one person knew where I was staying. I'd mentioned it to Belinda the other day because she seemed nervous about the case."

"It's not impossible to find someone," Marylin said. "All this is nonsense."

"I don't know. I think a jury would also be impressed with the fact that the photographer, Nauchbor, not only wasn't surprised to hear from someone representing you the other morning but let slip the fact that you'd called him earlier."

Marylin's face got very red and angry. "That proves nothing."

"But suggests everything. Publicity, contacts, news management—it's your big skill, Marylin, and this was nicely done. Anyone with a grain of sense will see it's a put-up job. And luckily for me, it worked smoothly. I could have lost an eye, been drowned—"

She protested.

"As it is, I was taken off a potentially very lucrative job and had my reputation for discretion damaged. I think I'm entitled to some compensation."

Belinda broke into nervous laughter. Marylin got up, stamped around the room, and finally began to dial—the police or her lawyer or a friend in the mob. All three possibilities were suggested, but, regrettably, I never discovered the lucky intended, because she chickened out at the very last minute when I said, "But the case involving me is nothing. It's murder and attempted murder you should worry about."

The phone clicked. Marylin was really a remarkable person. She had the ability to work herself up into a rage, then turn it off with the flick of a switch. She came back to the table and sat down as if she had never raised her voice. "Now we'll have a talk," she said, "while I decide whether to charge you with blackmail or libel."

"Such a lot of work for the legal profession," I said, "but you have no case. Listen: I can pretty well prove that you and Belinda attacked me in the hotel pool. You and I know that that was basically a stunt. Nicely handled, let me add, but almost too effective. Those blood-smeared *News* photos might suggest you also had something to do with Arthur McNab's unfortunate injury. Especially when you were right in Poughkeepsie the day it happened.''

Marylin sat up very straight and shot an angry look at Belinda. ''You fool,'' she said. ''What have you done?''

''It wasn't me. It wasn't! I told her it had nothing to do with us,'' Belinda cried in alarm.

''You can't deny you were there,'' I continued, ''because I can produce one witness and doubtless could find others.''

''You cannot bring this up,'' Marylin said in a tight, strained voice. ''You simply cannot use this.''

I ignored the warning; she had already given me so many. ''No? Why not? Whoever is linked to Arthur McNab's injury is very likely the person who killed your husband.''

For a moment Marylin was silent, as if considering this proposition curiously, before she said, ''My husband drowned. It is preposterous to suggest anything else. That idea is just a fiction of the insurance company's.''

''I'm not working for them anymore. You got me fired, remember? As a matter of fact, they weren't too keen on that theory, didn't see there was any support for it. So long as I was employed by them, I had to let it go.''

''You have nothing. You're just wasting my time and frightening Belinda.''

''Wrong. Your husband was murdered. Very cleverly. He was drowned after he suffered one of his seizures out on the jetty. The killer came along and rolled him into the water.''

Marylin's fingers began a nervous inventory of the

clutter and papers. "Henry didn't have seizures often," she said.

"He had a number of minor ones during the making of *The Lazarus Gambit*."

She shook her head and brushed the idea away with her hand as if it had been a cobweb or a persistent fly.

"That's why you didn't want me to see the outtakes, isn't it? It's quite clear in the film. Those segments have been sent up to Hartford. After the company doctors get through examining them, there'll be no doubt that your husband had been almost incapacitated by the disease. I don't think you've a prayer of attacking that evidence in court. You'd have done better to take your chances and leave me at work."

"You'd done enough damage already."

"With me it was double or nothing. I ruled out accident almost from the first. My hypothesis was that Henry Brook either committed suicide or was murdered. My investigations have ruled out the first possibility. So, Mrs. Brook, you still have the chance to collect on his policy. Unless you killed him."

"Why should I have killed him? Henry was my creation. Oh yes, you think 'another backstage wife.' Let me tell you: Henry had great talent but no idea of how to manage it. None whatsoever. No money sense, no business sense, no public relations sense. Was it an accident that a man like that became both a star and a great artist? Was it?"

"That doesn't answer the question, Mrs. Brook."

At this point, Belinda suddenly began to cry.

"Stop that," I said. "It was your suggestion originally."

"What have you been telling this woman?" Marylin demanded.

"I was only teasing," Belinda said in a childish voice. "You knew that, didn't you? I just made that up."

"Most people do not tease about accusing their guardian of murder."

Belinda jumped up and ran out of the room. Marylin shrugged as if this was unimportant or at least routine. "Belinda lies," she remarked. "I warned you about that."

"In that case, though, she might be telling the truth. You had a motive—two, in fact: your husband's insurance and his flagrant infidelities. You had the knowledge of his illness and of how it could be precipitated. You had as much opportunity as anyone at the party, or more. As circumstantial evidence, we have the facts that you attacked me to ensure that I would be removed from the insurance company's investigation and that you were in the vicinity the day Arthur McNab was nearly murdered."

"That's the weak spot," she said quickly. "Why should I have harmed the caretaker? There's no reason for that."

"Arthur McNab was attacked for the device that made the murder possible." I watched her face; she seemed genuinely surprised.

"There was no weapon. He drowned."

"I didn't say 'weapon'; I said 'device.' But only the killer knows about that." Behind me, Belinda had wandered back into the room, her white outfit a pale, subliminal blur in the mirror over the cluttered sideboard.

"Something that produced a seizure?"

I nodded.

"It is possible," she said at last. "It is—" Without warning, her head snapped back. She threw up her right hand and pushed away her chair. Behind me, there was a sound and I caught a metallic flash in the mirror. This time I didn't hesitate. I dived onto the floor as the knife hit the fine polished table with a high, reverberating thud. The bone-china cups and the crystal glasses rattled and rang, and Belinda brought the knife down again, scattering them, and again, gouging the table, and again, a passionate, meaningless repetition. I scuttled away and jumped to my feet, but Marylin walked calmly around the table and put her hand on Belinda's arm. She froze, then brought the knife down one last time, so hard it stuck, trembling in the mahogany, before Marylin led her to a chair and reached into a drawer for some pills. Belinda held out her hand.

"One," Marylin said, "and then you will go to your shooting."

Belinda swallowed but shook her head.

"A top model does not cancel appointments. You will phone and apologize. Then you will get a cab." Her voice was absolutely firm, almost mechanical.

"She's not to know," Belinda said. "She's not to know."

"You have been foolish," Marylin said with a glance of pure contempt at me, "but we will work something out. I know this type."

"You have to call my cab," Belinda said in her high, whiny child's voice. "I'll be late. There's my hair."

"You are fine." Marylin went to the telephone and badgered the cab dispatcher. Her sense of grievance was always available to her but always controlled. What I had taken for unthinking rudeness was calculation; the cab was promised. Marylin sat down at the table and lit a cigarette. Belinda remained in the chair in the corner, running her thumb along her fingers as if she'd like to bite her nails, and I returned to my seat without meeting her eyes. No one spoke. My stomach jumped as I studied the marks on the table, looked at the chef's knife poised like Excalibur just to the right of my coffee cup, and tried to remember exactly where I had been sitting and what part of my anatomy had been in the direct line. Arm? Hand? Shoulder? Back? Fear that comes tardily can be no less intense. I glanced at Marylin, sitting immobile, and Belinda, twisting her fingers over and over. What they thought of, I can't tell, for no one spoke for five, maybe even ten, minutes, until a horn sounded and we heard steps outside the door. Belinda jumped up, grabbed the tote bag, and ran eagerly for the bell as if the sound had been a signal, and the cabbie the enchanted huntsman arrived to release the spell.

"Thanks for coming. We'll have to rush. Battery Park, please, it's for some pictures." Then her feet pattered down the steps. Marylin Brook let out her breath slowly and suddenly looked very old. "Do you smoke?" she asked.

"I gave it up."

She poured the dregs of the coffee into her cup and picked one of the glasses out of the margarine dish.

"Is she seeing someone?" I asked.

"Yes. Twice a week. I arranged that. Henry would never have thought of it. She's been worse, of course, since his death. Hence these fantasies that I killed him."

"The little hotel episode can't have helped her, either, if what just happened is any indication."

"She was desperate. I thought we could manage it. Convince you, that is." Marylin sighed an angry, put-upon sigh. "You can blame me for that. I thought Belinda'd be all right if you left the case. I can't think of everything." She got up, looked for a clean ashtray, and set it down on the papers.

"What's wrong with her?"

Marylin shrugged. "Childhood, sex...the doctor says severe emotional disturbance. No sign of schizophrenia, thank God. Belinda's had a...difficult life."

"She's gotten herself into rather sophisticated company," I remarked.

"Henry met her at a party. He was always meeting people at parties, always thinking this was the magic person, the lost inspiration, his lost youth, whatever. Beware of romantic men." She shook her head.

"How'd she come to live with you?"

"As usual," Marylin said in a cool and business-like way, "I checked up on Henry's latest enthusiasm. When I discovered her age, I was alarmed, especially when I saw how troubled she was. It wasn't too hard to persuade her to break it off, but she had a price. Fortunately, she's proved to have some talent. For modeling, that is; I don't think Len Rossol will turn her into an actress."

"So she was allowed to move in and make a modeling career in exchange for dropping your husband."

"You have a certain felicitous brevity."

"I've been told one of the problems between your husband and Rossol was Belinda."

"Most certainly. Belinda is not so fond of sex as she is of power. Offscreen," Marylin said dryly, "she acted quite adequately."

"And what about her parents?"

"The mother is a fool."

"Belinda said she needed money."

"Oh, yes, but she knew how to get it." Marylin's mouth fell into a tight, sour line. "It is my opinion that she threw Belinda at Henry in order to—"

"—extort?"

"Extort funds for her next escapade. She's one of those women who has to have the very best—beautiful home, good address, designer clothes—but lacks sufficient skill to get it for herself. I didn't think that was the first time she'd made use of Belinda's extraordinary appearance, but I had no proof. If I had, things would have been different."

So I could imagine. "That doesn't explain why you were in Poughkeepsie or why Belinda kept making trips there."

"That had nothing to do with the case. You must take my word for it. Absolutely nothing."

"The charge, Mrs. Brook, is murder. There won't be a possibility of taking anyone's word for anything."

"She's hardly more than a child," Marylin said, jumping up nervously and puffing all the while on her cigarette. "She was fine, fine until all this. Even with her mother, with everything, she was remarkable. So mature, so sophisticated. Then we went upstate…"

There was real grief in her voice, and to my surprise, I realized that the vile-tempered Marylin Brook loved her husband's underage "enthusiasm."

"You think there's something comic about this," she said, as if reading my mind.

"I hadn't thought you cared about anyone." Bluntness seemed not to distress her.

"I was cut out for children," she said reflectively. Maybe that was true.

"Belinda's not exactly a child."

"But almost. She's deformed. Too grown up in a few ways, still infantile in others. That was why we went to Poughkeepsie. I wanted to give her back her childhood. She needed to experience the past, to come to terms with it." This was the old Marylin, expansive and high-flown, but now I could see the effort that kept her afloat.

"What was in Poughkeepsie?"

"I can't trust you with that."

"I'll find out one way or the other. Probably there will be less fuss if you tell me."

She hesitated.

"Do you understand how crucial this is? Without an explanation for your trips upstate, you are a very good suspect in both an attempted murder and a murder."

"And if I have an explanation, do you know who killed my husband?"

"Then I have someone else with motive, knowledge, and opportunity. Proof will come later. Perhaps with your assistance."

Marylin Brook looked thoughtful. I didn't hurry her and she began to walk back and forth along the floor,

setting it squeaking and creaking at all its joints. After
a few minutes she picked up the phone, dialed. "Yes,
it's Marylin Brook," she said. "Has Belinda arrived?
Unavoidable. I told her to go directly to the site. Yes,
yes, a super girl. All right, thanks. 'Bye." As she put
down the phone, Marylin said, "She seems to have
managed to get there all right."

"That's good." But I wondered if Belinda belonged in a pressure business of any kind.

"We went to see her father," she said quickly.

"Yes?"

"In Poughkeepsie, I mean. He lives there."

"Is that such a secret?"

"The mother left him years ago. He's a hopeless
alcoholic, but Belinda has always idealized him, the
absent daddy syndrome, you realize. When she came
east, she hired someone to find him. By unhappy coincidence, the information came just as we were leaving to go on location."

She lit another cigarette. "Belinda was wild with
joy. It was the first time I had ever seen a break in
that sophistication, in that numbness. Her mother
hadn't been able to take care of her, and she realized
that, but her father would. Everything would be different—that's what I mean by infantile," Marylin
added.

"And she was disillusioned?"

"He didn't remember her. He works part-time as a
college lecturer, in between bouts. I truly don't think
he did remember. She'd have been little more than an
infant. When he was sober, he was polite but apprehensive. She's the age of his youngest students, and
he suspected a prank."

"How did Belinda take this?"

"She was stunned. Absolutely astonished. And then, it was as if...as if something in her had been wiped out. I tried to explain, said to give him time, but she didn't know how to cope, didn't know how to approach him. She'd had no experience with men, you see, that is except as—"

"—as lovers?"

"It was never going to work out. I met him. He was a ridiculous man, like something out of a Russian novel, boring, incompetent, full of obscure miseries. Not the sort of father Belinda needed at all." Marylin's mouth drew into a tight line. Maybe she was right; maybe she had been cut out for children. She would have reordered the universe for them.

"Belinda didn't see it," she continued, "wouldn't see it. She pursued him; she was determined to have him recognize her. I had to tell the cast they were not to take her into town. I had to watch her for hitchhiking. The trips with Arthur seemed safe. They were not too long, and he was ultrareliable. If she was to be brought home, he'd see to it."

"So she didn't succeed?"

"She tried too hard. She managed to get into Poughkeepsie one evening. He only drank at night, I should add. She made a big scene and he made a pass at her. Of course, she was upset, hated him. That was the night before the party. Then the next evening, the very next evening, Henry drowned."

"A tough combination."

"She's fine unless there's any mention of Henry or those trips to Poughkeepsie. Then she either accuses me of killing him or goes into hysterics. As you saw.''

"What does her doctor say?''

"Guilt, transference, grief. Henry's dead; her father, as father, is dead. The woman pretends I'm to blame; the child believes she killed him.''

"And can she stay with you? I mean, is it possible?''

"There's no one else," Marylin said with dignity. "There is no one else competent. Her mother! Neither the brains nor the morals of a cat. And her father... He's not an evil man. He just can't cope. Never could, I imagine. And after what's happened, it would be tragic. No, it's got to be me," she concluded dramatically. "There's no one else who could handle it.''

Belinda would be the next Henry Brook, to be managed, indulged, and bullied. I wondered if Marylin would get any happiness from her efforts and her unpleasant but nonetheless perfectly genuine devotion. Her hard, strong face suggested probably not. She turned to me and said, "I've told you. Now you tell me. Who killed my husband?''

I opened my case and produced the flasher. "This is what killed your husband.''

"They use that in the studio. It's a sort of light switch.''

"Close. It's called a flasher and it makes lights—''

"I know! I know!" she cried, "and we thought it was heat lightning!''

I must have looked surprised, for she continued in a rush. "At the party, when the lights flickered once or twice. Out on the jetty.''

"Yet you didn't worry when Henry was late getting back?"

"I was too concerned about Belinda. She didn't tell me what had happened until one of the crew made a remark at the party about her going into town and coming back with her hair mussed. We went right to our rooms. She was terribly upset."

It was just possible. "But the lights. No one thought to mention them."

"No one there knew of Henry's illness but me."

I shook my head. "Two other people knew. The younger Mr. Delf knew from his parents. And he'd told Len Rossol."

Marylin went white. "He told Len?"

"Yes."

"Before?"

I nodded.

She stood up, one hand supporting her weight against the table, and I thought there would be a great, dramatic explosion of grief. Her jaw was set, her eyes flashed; try as I might, I could not see Marylin as anything but a theatrical figure. But again she surprised me. I must admit that of all the odd characters both literary and real around *The Lazarus Gambit*, Marylin Brook was the most complex and surprising. She turned to me and leaned over the table. "You can do it," she said. "You can nail that bastard. I'll pay you anything you want to see it's done."

FOURTEEN

ALTHOUGH I DECLINED Marylin Brook's generous offer, I enlisted her support, and, after she was dressed, I dropped her off to join Belinda. Then I returned to my hotel, checked that Valon was at the home office, and called Harry. My domestic fences took so long to mend that it was well after ten o'clock before I settled my bill and close to one-thirty before I squeezed into a parking space in Hartford.

Independence Mutual's home office was a palace of industry in the old style, with a fine limestone facade ornamented by Corinthian columns and a low dome, which fronted a sweeping circular entrance and magnificent grounds. The lawns were luxuriously green, their weedless expanse broken by splendid copper beeches and small groves of evergreens. A fortune in pachysandra blanketed the shadows, and I could see a pair of gardeners at work in tulip beds arranged with military precision. Outside the stone and ironwork that separated this commercial Elysium from the street, a vendor was selling an assortment of indigestibles. I bought a concoction smothered in chili sauce that dripped cheese, onions, and lettuce and sat down contentedly on the wall.

This was not the proper approach to the halls of Independence Mutual, but I didn't care. Forty million dollars of their money was on the line, and if I felt like a picnic on the lawn they would just have to put up with it.

"I'll take an ice cream bar too, please," I told the vendor.

"You're the only one not on a diet today. This weather, you'd think the ices would move, wouldn't ya?"

"Yes, you would. How much?"

"Depends on what you want. Regular is two dollars. The double almond's this week's special. You can get that for a buck-fifty."

"The special will be fine," I said, handing over a bill. I was thinking that even one percent of forty million dollars came to a lot of money—enough to capitalize Executive Security very adequately. And while Independence Mutual would balk at handing over any such sum, they would scarcely be able to challenge *The Lazarus Gambit* claim without the contents of my briefcase. Success would simply be a matter of selecting the right approach, and fortunately a misspent youth had given me a certain expertise in, as well as a taste for, quasilegitimate negotiations.

At the end of the drive, I walked up a big flight of steps and opened a bronze door to the domed rotunda. Presiding over this impressive space was a sleek receptionist sitting at a bare rosewood desk like an expensive artifact. Her voice had the soft portentiousness of a mortuary attendant's. "Perhaps I can get a message to Mr. Valon if it's really vital," she whispered, "but he is in a very important committee meeting."

"Tell him it concerns *The Lazarus Gambit* settlement, not the Brooks' policy. I have just come in from

New York, and it is absolutely essential that everything be settled this afternoon.''

She conducted complex negotiations on the phone with Valon's assistant secretary, then his personal secretary. There was a pause. "He'll be out of the meeting in a quarter of an hour," she announced at last, "if you'd just wait."

I sat down in a comfortable leather chair. Twenty minutes later, a spruced-up young man with embalmed hair, a Florida tan, and a brisk, self-important manner appeared. "Ted Jamison," he announced, holding out his hand. "I'm Alex Valon's assistant."

"How do you do?"

"I'm afraid Mr. Valon's going to be tied up for a time. If there's anything I could handle…"

I was getting tired of company protocol. "I must either see Mr. Valon now, or I will take the matter up with the Board of Directors."

"That's impossible."

"I think not. The possibility of paying out millions on *The Lazarus Gambit* claim is surely a matter that has attracted the board's attention. I asked to see Mr. Valon only as a courtesy—which he scarcely deserves after having taken me off the case. If it's too much trouble for him to see me, I don't mind dealing directly with the people in charge."

"They're all very busy. Had you made an advance appointment—"

"Mr. Jamison, *I'm* very busy. If Independence Mutual would rather not save its stockholders a large sum of money, I think I'll just save myself some time."

I'd only gotten a few feet toward the doors when Jamison leapt to my elbow. "Perhaps you'd better come up to our office so we can discuss this," he said, his expression wavering between doubt and annoyance.

"With Mr. Valon."

He hesitated.

"I can guarantee he'll be delighted to see me," I said. "You don't have to worry about that."

Jamison led the way to the elevators, snapped at the operator, and stood at corporate attention without giving me another glance. Clearly, I was not a welcome prodigal, and upstairs, in a cozy wood-paneled arrangement that hinted quite successfully at old money, there was another wait and another conference before Alex himself appeared, his anger suppressed by his habitual good manners.

"Ms. Peters," he said, without shaking hands. "I thought I made it clear during our last talk that you were off the case entirely. I can't understand why you've come. I've just been called out of a very important meeting. What's this about?"

"Something at least as important as your meeting. You might ask your assistant to make an appointment for us to talk to the president or to the director of the board. In twenty minutes, maybe?"

Valon looked embarrassed, as if he had inadvertently brought someone wildly unsuitable to an important party. "Really, this is impossible. Ted, if you'd show Ms. Peters downstairs. I told you—"

"Henry Brook was murdered."

There was a sudden silence. Even the typist stopped, her nimble hands poised over her keyboard.

"We'd better discuss this inside." Valon opened the door and stood grim-faced while I entered.

"Will you need me, sir?" Jamison asked.

"Not now." He shut the door with as close to a slam as I'd imagine Valon ever allowed himself.

"Well," he said, lowering himself stiffly into his chair, "you'd better explain yourself."

I took my time pulling up a seat. "Henry Brook was murdered. His drowning was neither an accident nor a suicide but murder one—planned, premeditated, deliberate. This is not a theory, this is a fact."

"Can you prove that?"

"I have brought the proof with me."

"Well! This is all very sudden, Anna," he said, changing his tune and beginning to fuss with his papers and his fine lacquer pen. "Perhaps I owe you an apology."

"You do owe me an apology, but I'm sure my removal from the case was not solely your idea."

"No, there were some repercussions, as you might imagine. Going outside the company for an investigator aroused certain ill feelings in our department. It's just not the way Independence Mutual has traditionally managed things."

"And so you're in hot water?"

"In a manner of speaking."

"Then I'm bringing good news, but not, I'm afraid, for your particular department. If I am right about this, Brook's policy will need to be paid; the entire *Lazarus Gambit* claim, however, will perhaps be saved."

Valon leaned back in his chair. "You're talking very big figures."

"Nonetheless, I have reason. I know how Brook

was murdered and I have the device that killed him."
I patted my briefcase.

"With you? You should have turned that over to
the police."

"Certainly, but since I had been employed by the
company to look into the matter, I felt an obligation
to inform you first, especially since I'm told the check
is to be turned over next week."

"Even though you'd been taken off the case?" Valon was surprised but also cautious.

"I chose to regard that as words spoken in anger.
Clients for my sort of business are often nervous and
difficult."

"I see. Well, normally I could not approve of that
sort of assumption but under the circumstances..."
He nodded his head, obviously relieved.

"Our agreement, of course, will have to be rene-
gotiated." I smiled but Valon's barely restored cor-
diality withered. "I was fired, after all. I needn't tell
you that the loss of a position of trust with Independence Mutual will make problems for me profession-
ally."

Valon fussed about this for a time, then said,
"You're absolutely sure about Brook, are you?"

"I have no doubts whatsoever."

"It's a good thing you informed us," he said unhappily, "but I am not authorized to decide any new
terms."

"That was the reason I suggested we speak to the
president or to the board."

Valon went to the outer office. In a surprisingly
short time he returned with the information that we
had been summoned and that if the great man was

satisfied with my report, we would be joined by the several board members available that afternoon. He led the way down a wide, somber hall, worn by the passage of generations of actuaries, to the presidential suite.

Like Valon's domain, these offices were comfortable and impressive without being flashy. We were greeted by a handsome older woman who pressed the intercom, announced our arrival, and gave me a jaundiced look, which confirmed the suspicion that I was beginning to look rather the worse for wear.

"Mr. Woodward will see you now, Mr. Valon."

She opened the door and ushered us into another fine office, this one with a quite magnificent view over the company's grounds to the city beyond. There were large bookcases on two sides, filled exclusively with company reports, beginning with dark and crumbling leather-bound ledgers from the earliest days and running unbroken to the modern era of green vinyl on the lower right. The appalling monotony of this collection suggested some very rigorous brand of self-mortification, an impression immediately strengthened by R. Cecil Woodward, sitting thin and motionless beneath the whiskered portraits of two of his predecessors like a sage beneath his icons.

The president was small and so neatly made as to seem almost delicate. He had a fine head with beautiful cheekbones and a high, smooth forehead, pale, faintly slanted eyes, and a wide, still, thin-lipped mouth. His face was austere and somehow ascetic, and I felt a little nervous anxiety immediately succeeded by curiosity as to what had secured the concentration that so marked his features.

"How do you do?" he said, extending his hand. "This comes as a surprise. Alex had assured me that you had withdrawn from the case."

"There have been certain surprising developments, Mr. Woodward."

"So I understand. Do sit down. Margaret," he said to his secretary, "I'd like you to stay and take notes." When she was settled, he turned to me. "Now, Ms. Peters, if you would care to begin."

I gave Woodward a rapid summary of the case, omitting such details as Rossol's little prank and Belinda's hysteria, and explaining the factors that had made me wary, first of the official account and, later, of the idea of a spontaneous seizure. "It had crossed my mind after seeing the film outtakes—they reached here safely?"

"They did indeed. Thank you."

"Anyway, those outtakes suggested that someone with a knowledge of Brook's condition might consider manipulating it."

"Our doctors assure us, by the way, that that is quite possible."

"I am not surprised. There was, however, no proof that that had been done until now. As I told Mr. Valon, I have recovered the device that triggered Brook's fatal attack."

"Are we to see this interesting item?" Woodward asked coolly.

"When certain other things have been discussed."

"Such as?"

"First, I think you will agree that such evidence is of the foremost importance to your company."

Woodward leaned back in his chair and folded his

thin, white hands on top of his desk piously. "It would be of interest to the police," he said, "but how does it help us, Ms. Peters? If Brook was murdered, we must pay on his policy. If his murder prevented the completion and distribution of *The Lazarus Gambit,* we are liable for the costs of the production."

"But it all depends, does it not, on the identity of the killer?"

Woodward's face took on a peculiar intensity of expression, and I was disillusioned to see that nothing more extraordinary than money lay behind that remarkable concentration of energy. The thought of saving the *Gambit* settlement made him smile in the midst of this rather macabre discussion. "Only one person will do," he said. "Then we could consider this murder a case of fraud."

"With careful police work I'm sure there would have been no question."

"But there was not careful police work," he responded snappishly, "and what the local constable and the state troopers will make of the interesting device you mentioned must remain in doubt."

"With the rest of my information, plus a tape I have, they could make a good deal. In addition, I think more testimony can be obtained. And possibly an eyewitness."

"Really!" Valon exclaimed.

"Of course," I continued, "this is risky and time-consuming work. As I explained to Mr. Valon, we will have to renegotiate our agreement."

Woodward's clear eyes became a trifle cloudy. "You will have to discuss that with Alex. Some com-

pensation for your extra work, although it was clearly
not authorized by the company, is probably in order.''

"I'm afraid what I have to propose must be discussed with you.''

"I can't think why,'' he said, his voice bland.

"Because I think a percentage would be right. Say
one percent of your savings on *The Lazarus Gambit*
policy if the company doesn't have to pay off.''

"Do you realize how much money that is?''

"It's fairly simple arithmetic, Mr. Woodward.''

The austere face grew colder and more crafty.
"Such an arrangement is quite out of the question.
I'm afraid you have no choice but to accept our reg-
ular fee schedule.''

"Why is that?''

"Because, with time, we can discover the information, Ms. Peters. We can simply stall the film company until we have retraced your steps. I think you'll
find that Independence Mutual can outwait you.''

"But not Len Rossol. His studio has been promised
the check. Whatever suspicions you may now have,
you have no proof without my evidence.''

"Your evidence may not give us the right
killer—by that, I mean the one that will save us from
having to settle.''

That was bald enough. "No,'' I admitted.

"Then for what, Ms. Peters, would we be paying
you such an outrageous sum?''

"For my knowledge and professional skill. I believe there was a witness. I know who that is and how
to secure the information we want. I also believe I
know what would put sufficient pressure on Rossol to
decide the matter one way or another.''

"Kindly remember that unless he did it, we are liable for over forty million dollars."

"And I am out over four hundred thousand dollars. It's a gamble, but that's what the insurance business is about, isn't it?"

There was some discussion on this and a call for one of the company lawyers. Then the chairman of the board was summoned and everything was hashed over again.

"We can delay this," Woodward insisted, "then we can take the matter to court and subpoena Ms. Peters."

"So you can," I said in disgust. "In the meantime, Rossol's lawyers would be delighted to take custody of the device and any other evidence. Doubtless, they would be able to come up with a variety of alternate explanations to muddy the waters."

There was an outcry at this suggestion, and my refusal to be cheated caused a few of those present to take personal offense. I was accused of a number of unattractive things, including obstruction of justice and greed. Fortunately, I held some good cards, and when I finally suggested that three-quarters of a percent for success or my usual retainer for days worked if the case was not proved might be adequate, there was a sudden willingness to compromise. The lawyers sketched an agreement, Woodward's formidable secretary typed copies, and by the time the commuter traffic beyond Independence Mutual's green lawns had thinned to a trickle, we had signed our respective names.

"Well?" Woodward demanded.

I opened my briefcase and placed the flasher on his desk. "This is what killed Henry Brook."

"What is it?" Woodward asked, turning the device over in his hands curiously.

"It's a flasher."

"I beg your pardon."

"That's what it's called. It's an electrical device, which, when wired into a circuit, causes lights to flash. The company reported one missing just after Brook's death, but Arthur McNab, the caretaker, had forgotten about it until the other day when he saw it in use in the village."

"So this has since been tested?" Valon asked.

"That's right. The fellow who took the flasher had rigged it up to a tavern sign. Although it worked perfectly, it caused the lights to flash at an uncomfortably fast rate even for perfectly normal persons."

"That certainly would lend support to your theory."

"Yes, it does. And Davies's testimony—he's the fellow who took the flasher—is interesting as well. Shall I play it for you now?"

"By all means," said Woodward. "We want our money's worth."

I ignored this sally and switched on the machine. When the tape was done, I said, "I spoke with Marylin Brook today and she confirmed his testimony. The jetty lights apparently did flicker, but those in the pavilion attributed the flashes to heat lightning. No one seems to have been puzzled or at all concerned."

"Surely few if any of them knew of Brook's condition?"

"Three of them did, possibly four. Mrs. Brook, of course, Jim Delf, who learned from his parents—"

"I think we can rule him out," Woodward said, closing ranks with his own caste.

"I do too, although he'd had a quarrel with Brook only a week or so before. It seems that in retaliation, he revealed Brook's secret to the director, Len Rossol."

Woodward looked as though he considered this move in the worst taste. "You mentioned a fourth person?"

"I suspect that Belinda Tayana, the young model who was living with Brook and his wife, also knew, though I cannot confirm this."

"These people were all at the party?"

"That's right, and Delf, because it was his home, and the film people, because they were familiar with electrical circuits, would all have been able to tamper with the wiring for the party decorations."

"And you believe one of these individuals altered the circuits in order to provoke Brook's seizure?"

"Correct."

"A nice piece of detection," the company lawyer said. "I can't imagine why none of this was turned up earlier."

"Incompetence in law enforcement from top to bottom," Woodward said. "This is all impressive, and expensive, detection, but it still doesn't save our bacon."

"The company has promised Rossol his money for early next week?"

"That's right. Everything should be ready Wednesday."

"As it turns out, that's the day he and quite a few members of the cast and crew are to return to the Delf estate. They plan to shoot a few scenes in the pavilion and on the jetty as an introduction for the documentary he wants to make out of *The Lazarus Gambit* footage."

"A very questionable proceeding," Woodward remarked.

"I thought," I continued, "that it would be wise for some Independence Mutual people to be on hand to present the check and record the transaction. Perhaps it would make a nice little piece for your company bulletin; you know, 'Company Settles Record Film Production Claim.' You'll want a photographer on hand."

"Ms. Peters, that is not the way we normally do business." said Woodward.

"This is not your usual settlement. This somewhat theatrical approach will enable us to re-create the scene at the party, and that, ladies and gentlemen, will allow us to tap a resource that has not been previously used."

"And what is that?" the lawyer asked.

"I'd prefer for you to wait and see. In the meantime, this is for you to turn over to the proper authorities." I indicated the tape. "A written report of my other investigations will be on your desk before Wednesday," I told Woodward. "If we are successful, you will be able to destroy that check for the film company losses."

Woodward thought for a moment, then spoke to his secretary. "Margaret, you will make the arrangements. And include someone from the PR department. A photographer, you say?''

"Or an artist. If there's no one suitable, I know someone who would do nicely, and provide a bit of muscle if that should be required.''

Woodward's face grew hard. "Is there a need for that?''

"There might be. Arthur McNab's injuries were potentially very serious, and I needn't point out my own little 'accident.'''

"We do not want any further injuries—or any Wild West antics, either.''

"I will take care of that.''

"I trust you are not taking on more than you can manage, Ms. Peters,'' he said dryly. "The consequences for you, aside from your own financial losses, could be unpleasant.'' His expression left me in no doubt about the powers of a firm like Independence Mutual nor his willingness to use them. I was tempted to ask if this was what he meant by "the company's way of doing business'' but refrained.

"I understand,'' I said, feeling euphoric. "I'm sure you'll be completely satisfied.''

FIFTEEN

"I JUST CAN'T IMAGINE IT," Harry said for the second or third time and shook his head regretfully. "He's one of the great film talents of the last twenty years."

"It may not be him. I've told you that. Damn likely but not certain." I stared out at the sun-drenched pastureland, where slow trails of black-and-white cows grazed. Although he usually regards such outings as adventures, Harry had not been at all pleased to come north. Indeed, I was beginning to wonder if artistic solidarity might not prove stronger than legal considerations. "After all, Henry Brook was quite a talent."

"We could be losing both of them. Isn't that worse? I don't see why you couldn't have gotten Garret for this."

"Garret's a free-lance. He's on a temp doing bodyguard duty."

"Oh, yeah?" Harry asked. Both Garret and his peculiar profession seemed to have captured his imagination. "Where?"

"I don't know. The usual—some dictator's nephew or film star's kid."

"Too bad. He could have driven up here."

"This isn't a job for Garret. He thinks a camera is for concealing poisoned darts. He's small but lethal. What's needed today is size."

"Oh, thanks."

"And brains."

"Actually," he said, somewhat mollified, "Garret seems a good sort."

"If this works out, I may be able to hire him full-time." But even this reference to the insurance deal was a mistake, because Harry lapsed again into gloom. "Look at the scenery," I said with forced enthusiasm. "Would you rather be cooped up in the city?"

"Lots of cows."

"What's wrong with cows? Who was it, Millet? Landseer? Got a lot of mileage out of cows."

"Landseer! You're as bad as Jan, bringing back all that High Victorian kitsch," he said indignantly, and I remembered that he and his partner had recently had a fine squabble about the merits of the Victorians. Clearly, it was to be one of those days when I couldn't say anything right. I slouched in the seat, let the silence lengthen, and thought uneasily about the deficiencies of my plan. Rossol might prove cagey; the cast might be resistant; some nice people could get hurt. Strategic confrontations are exciting, but they can get you into awfully deep water.

"What are you nervous about?" Harry asked after a while.

"Nothing. I'm not nervous about anything."

"Have it your way. You've just seemed a little grumpy."

I could feel myself starting to get angry. "Who's grumpy?"

"Well, I am too," he said with the sweet reasonableness that is sometimes as annoying as bad temper. "But you know why I'm out of sorts."

I didn't say anything for a minute. It was true; I

was nervous. "I'm worried about Gloria," I said. "She's the person who does continuity. If anyone can remember anything significant, she's the one."

"Maybe she won't be there."

"Oh, she'll be there. She never moves from Rossol's side. That's her problem. Besides, she's working on the documentary."

"So what's the difficulty?"

"She seems nice, and she adores Rossol. If my idea works, she'll be miserable."

"Better than leaving her working for our mad-dog director," he said sarcastically.

"He's not mad, just ruthless. He wanted the studio; Brook's antics threatened to take it from him." I shrugged. "It's perfectly simple and completely inexplicable."

"I'm rooting for the wife," Harry said.

"Preferring to find your murderer in the bosom of the family? There would be problems with her, too. Slow down ahead. That's the road to the village."

"You were right about it being Black Foresty," Harry said grudgingly.

"That and half a dozen other things. The diner in the center is all-American. From there on, the architecture runs the gamut."

We passed the post office, a clutch of stores, and the single traffic light, then turned onto the country road. When we reached the estate, I asked Harry to stop at the McNab's cottage, where I had a brief consultation with Arthur before we drove on to the main house. Valon had arrived before us; he was standing in the driveway, anxiously smoking a cigarette. "Oh, you're here at last. Good to see you, Anna," he said, his nervousness betraying him into unaccustomed informality.

"This is Harry Radford, my husband. He will be taking the pictures."

"Good, good. Everything seems in order."

"The cast and crew here?"

"Since six this morning, I'm told. I began to be afraid you'd miss them."

"Rossol won't leave without his check."

"If it's to be his." Valon wiped his damp forehead and reached into his car for a panama hat.

"We'd better get started, then. You brought Exhibit A?"

Valon handed over the package, and I put it in my case. "We've discussed what's to be done. I think everything should be clear."

"As it will ever be," he replied unhappily.

"Ready, Harry?"

My husband draped two cameras and a bag of film around his neck and nodded.

"Just one last thing: if any of our suspects want to leave, I mean suddenly, precipitously, don't try to stop them. That's important."

"Why on earth not?" Valon asked, and Harry look puzzled.

"I've lined up an additional and rather special witness. Okay?"

"This is all new to me," said Valon, and he fell into step beside Harry with a doleful expression. They kept trying to start a conversation, with so little success that I began to wish that Valon had stayed in Hartford, and Harry in D.C. When we came below the screening level of the trees, we saw the crew busy with their sunscreens, lights, and cameras beside the dock. The case was standing about in little groups, bored but patient, while Rossol bellowed directions, and Marylin Brook sat off to one side kibbutzing with Belinda and looking like an understudy for Madame Defarge. We stopped out of camera range to watch Lani Dupres, dressed in period costume and carrying a picnic hamper, walk along the jetty to a rowboat. When she reached her marks, she stopped, put down the basket, took off her sun hat, and began speaking: "...at the lake in upper New York State where many of *The Lazarus Gambit* scenes were filmed. Henry Brook and I worked here, and this lake is where he died."

"Cut," Rossol yelled. "Beautiful, Lani. All right. I think we have enough."

Some of the crew had noticed our approach, and Rossol called, "Well, boys and girls, here comes the insurance company." He avoided my eyes.

"This is Alex Valon from the life insurance division of Independence Mutual's home office. And this is Harry Radford, a graphic artist and photographer."

"We're getting the full treatment."

"This is quite an occasion," Valon said without much conviction. "The company thought it would make an interesting story for our internal publications."

"Explain to the stockholders, eh? Be my guest. The more publicity, the better the chances for the documentary. Believe me, old Independence Mutual can't lose on this one."

He called the cast forward to meet Valon and Harry. Remembering her from some obscure picture, my husband immediately struck up a conversation with Lani Dupres.

"I'm afraid we interrupted you," Valon said, anxious to postpone any confrontation. "Please go ahead."

Rossol checked his light meter. "We could shoot one more bit before we pack it in for the day. If you don't mind."

"I don't know about Mr. Radford, but I'd be fascinated," Valon said.

"Fine with me," said Harry.

My preferences were not consulted. I made my way over to Gloria to find out what they were doing.

"It's background for the voice-over. Len's going to read the script for now, so we can get an idea of the pacing." Rossol waved to her and she hurried away with her notebook as the crew got into position. The actors, now finished, scattered to change, to smoke, or, in the case of Lani Dupres, to gossip with the visitors, until Harry remembered his role and dutifully began snapping pictures. The film camera began to run. From my vantage point a little way up the hill, I could only hear snatches of the narration. "...the mystery of art and death...his inspired playing of the doomed Dr. Kleinz...the loss of a great actor leaves a darkness in the theater..." It struck me as a little pretentious, but then Rossol, for all his gifts, was not a great performer. He closed with the beautiful speech from *The Tempest* that ends, "We are such stuff as dreams are made of and our little lives are rounded with a sleep," getting a burst of applause from the cast. Valon whispered that he was relieved the production would be "tasteful," Harry said the lighting effects looked brilliant, and Rossol took a bow and hinted it was time for the check. Valon opened his mouth, but I interrupted. "I liked your speech, especially the part about the mystery of art."

Rossol gave me a wary look.

"Yes, I liked your connections between art and knowledge," I went on. "The idea that art can uncover mysteries."

Marylin had joined the little group. "Henry always said the best ideas just appeared, like magic."

"There is perhaps something magical. Or prescient. You were making that point, weren't you, Len, in the lines you gave Lani? I mean, about how sensitively Brook played the doomed Dr. Kleinz."

I thought Rossol's eyes were suspicious, but I had not misjudged him; work was his consuming passion, and he could not resist expounding his ideas to an enthusiastic audience.

"Interesting you should pick that up. I thought investigators were always very cut and dried—soil samples, schedule times, blood types."

"Until one sees great artists at work," I said.

I feared I had laid it on too heavily, but Rossol was off. He described his plans for the documentary and for the creation of a sense of mystery and fatality and discussed the attractions of the original plot, "pulp with redemption" as he called it. He believed serious themes could be embodied in popular culture, adding that that was one of the views he had shared with Brook. I noticed Marylin looked skeptical and a little contemptuous, and though the rest were enthralled, Belinda, too, seemed less than enchanted. She was sitting on the dock, throwing pebbles into the water, making me think Marylin had been unwise to bring her. Then Len paused a moment in his exposition, and I felt it was time.

"You're right," I said. "Completely. But, of course, some of this mystery could be cleared up."

Valon went a little gray, and all the others turned their attention to me except Belinda, who was still gazing dreamily over the sunny water.

"I'd say we had all the ingredients—an artist, actors, an investigator, a writer, and director—to solve your mystery at least as far as the party went."

"That sounds bizarre," said Marylin. "Charades are out. All this visiting the scene reminds me of the network stuff."

Bless her cantankerous heart. I could see Rossol was irked. He loved being center stage; he loved managing, organizing, and manipulating almost as much as Marylin did, and he was even more used to giving orders. "Not a charade," he said, probably against his better judgment, "a re-creation, an artistic re-creation." Emphasis on "artistic." I was interested to see what he would contrive.

"Something like that," I replied. "Your documentary is a start, but am I right in thinking that it is to deal only with the *Lazarus Gambit* script?"

"Except for coming here," Rossol said. "We had to show the end. Sorry, Marylin, but Henry would have wanted it. He never could resist the big scenes."

"Henry, at least, knew how to manage his big scenes," Marylin said.

"Darling, of course! He was a genius." Rossol turned and beamed at the cast. "Let's go inside. Using the party really is an idea. Yes, we could begin with our original plan, the South American village, then show the making of the film and end with some footage at the party site. With everyone knowing what's to happen.''

"One person knew last time," said Marylin.

Engrossed in his idea, Rossol either didn't hear her or ignored the remark. "We'd have to light the summerhouse very brightly—lanterns, strings of lights, everything—and the last shot would need to be from a barge, pulling back, pulling back with the summerhouse glittering on the water. A perfect image of the theater," he added delightedly, "glitter and warmth against a deep black night." As he spoke, his voice, which was not particularly beautiful, took on resonance. He had the genius of enthusiasm, and the cast responded to his excitement.

Especially Lani. "That's wonderful," she exclaimed. "And you're right about the theater. The stage! I never realized until I started with *Vaudeville Babes*—"

"Christ," said Marylin.

"We've got to get in," Rossol declared, looking around. "Is Delf here? No? Someone run and get that caretaker fellow."

I didn't want that. "Who knows where he'll be?" I said. "Better let me see what I can do."

Though my husband gave me a black look, I produced my lockpick and gave the ancient catch on the summerhouse door a rattle. "Voilà."

They clattered in, the crew throwing up high, dusty windows to let in the heat and the smell of blossoms. The summerhouse brought back the picnic shelters of my youth—cool, faintly musty spaces smelling of unpainted wood and leftover beer. A few streamers still fluttered from the rafters, and a paper cup crunched underfoot.

"There was a lot of music," said Lani. "Blondie, wasn't it?"

"And lots of booze," said a grip.

"The table was here," said my friend Alfred Hauer, aka Himmler.

There was a general milling around, with Rossol expounding, Marylin complaining, and Lani striking various attitudes. The crew was sent here and there on errands, Harry resumed snapping pictures, and Valon asked me in a hoarse whisper if I really thought this was a good idea. Someone turned on a powerful radio, and Rossol said, "Everyone was dancing at—what time shall we start?"

"Henry was here at eleven," said Marylin.

"He was talking to me," said Lani.

"Oh, ho," someone said.

"An artistic discussion," she corrected, very much on her dignity, and tossed her head. That was a new mannerism, probably adopted for *Vaudeville Babes.*

"I was drinking," said Alfred.

"With the beauteous Altheia," added one of the grips.

I noticed Belinda come quietly into the room.

"And I was standing in the corner talking to Gloria," Rossol said.

A little frown crossed Gloria's plain, sensitive face, and I saw her fingers tighten on her notebook.

"We're wasting time," I said. "We should ask the expert."

They were surprised, and Rossol's face betrayed a faint annoyance.

"What expert?" Marylin asked. "As far as I know, there are no experts on cast parties."

"Gloria, I'm sure, remembers everything," I said. "It's just like a scene, isn't it? You can remember. Who was where?"

"That's unreasonable," Rossol said. "Gloria was off duty. Continuity takes a lot of concentration."

"Best memory in the business," I said and hated myself when she smiled.

"Well," she began shyly, "Len was in the corner—no, a little further over. Lani was talking to Henry, that's right, but they were on the other side of the table—set right."

Automatically, Lani moved into position and, though he didn't like it, Len Rossol did too.

"You wanted to dance," Gloria said to Alfie, "but Altheia was tired. She went outside by the backdoor."

"Story of my life," Alfie joked.

Gloria was not distracted. She turned slowly, surveying the room with an expression of intense concentration. "Mrs. Brook, you were standing near the door, talking with Belinda. Then Len beckoned her, and she broke off the discussion and walked away." As she spoke, Gloria moved across the floor, adding, "Because I was dancing with Carl, I could see the entire room."

One of the men nodded. "That's right. I was showing some of my old disco moves."

The others laughed good-naturedly, but Gloria's face remained serious, and she gradually drew the others into her mood, particularly Belinda, who was

watching silently from the doorway. "Len and Belinda talked about something. She was on his right,
teasing him. She put her hand on his arm," Gloria
said, miming the action, "then she crossed to Lani
and Henry."

Belinda's face flushed and as rapidly grew pale.
"This is upsetting me, and I know it's upsetting Be-
linda," Marylin said, putting her arm around the girl's
shoulders. But Belinda, always surprising, giggled.
"Len wanted to play a little joke on Henry. He said
I should arrange to meet him out on the jetty."

Marylin turned to look at her, shocked and a little
frightened.

"God, Belinda! You misinterpret everything,"
Rossol exclaimed. "We were all going to cut out,
remember? Then you changed your mind, so I took
over playing the records."

Gloria shook her head. "That was later," she corrected. "No, you stayed where you were. Belinda
walked"—she gestured to show the direction—"and
whispered something to Henry."

"Rather rudely," Lani observed.

"I think you started to dance," Gloria said to Belinda. "You were laughing and joking, but I thought
you wanted to cry. Then you went outside. Henry
disappeared a moment later. We began dancing again,
but I was watching you, Len." There was a little edge
to her voice, the mark of disappointment in a gentle
nature.

"As usual," someone muttered.

"I was at the record player," Rossol repeated.
"Sometimes I think your memory isn't what it's
cracked up to be."

"You've never said that," Gloria exclaimed, hurt. "But I do remember exactly. It is just like a movie. Set right," she gestured toward Lani. "Set left, Max and Peter and a few others. Center, crowded with dancers. Table, center rear, Alfie—"

"Listen, Gloria, there were over a hundred people at that damn party," Rossol protested. "It was bedlam. That's why no one noticed when Henry disappeared. The police questioned everyone. There were half a dozen different times for when he left."

"They didn't ask me," Gloria said, "and anyway, it was different then. This is here, we're on the set. I never forget anything once I'm on the set. That's true, isn't it?" She appealed to the rest. Some nodded noncommittally; others looked away, unwilling to be drawn into what threatened to become a personal quarrel.

"I saw you go out," she said to Rossol with sudden anger. "Yes, Belinda left, then Henry. Then you."

"Ridiculous," Rossol said. "So who was playing the records?"

"You weren't gone long. Don't you remember? That was when the lightning started."

Marylin's face went rigid, but Gloria continued, innocent of the effect. "It was pretty, flickering over the water like a natural strobe light."

"Did Henry come back after the lightning?" I asked.

"No. I saw Belinda and Len, but I never saw Henry—"

"That means nothing," Rossol snapped. "You were probably making out with someone."

"It wasn't my fault," Belinda cried now, her voice

high and thin with fear. "It was only a joke. I was to tell him I'd hidden something out on the jetty for him. That's all. But I'm sure that wasn't when it happened. I'm sure. I'm sure Henry came back after that. Len told me. He told me it had to have happened later." Her eyes were panicky.

"Of course he came back. What's the matter with you, Gloria? You're just upsetting the kid. And this lightning business. You don't know what you're talking about. That's the trouble with cast parties—everyone gets high, everyone screws around and lies the next day." He laughed, but no one joined in.

"What's the matter, Len?" Gloria asked anxiously. "I wasn't high. Other people saw the lightning. It was warm. 'Unseasonable,' everyone said; that's why there was heat lightning. That's all. It's not so important, is it?" she appealed. "Is it, Len?"

"Shut the fuck up, Gloria. You don't know what you're talking about. One last time: Henry was here until midnight. I handled the records, and Belinda had one of her crises and ran off to bed."

"That's not true," Gloria said, her voice rising. She was frightened but persistent—or persistent because she was frightened. "If the others said that, they're wrong, because I remember. And there was lightning."

Everyone began to talk at once about this, then Belinda gave a little cut-off scream and burst into sobs. "Stop it," said Marylin. "Stop it!" Then she turned to Rossol. "You bastard, you killed my husband."

The crowd froze, appalled.

"You heard me. You got him out on the jetty—

you got Belinda to do that—you tricked her, tricked him. Then you killed him.''

"Marylin, sweetie, you've gone around the bend. I see this little experiment was a mistake, bad vibrations, bad karma. An artistic venture ill-fated from the start. You can feel the—''

"Bullshit,'' replied Marylin.

"You're making a mistake. You don't want to push this, Marylin—''

"Please, ladies and gentlemen,'' Valon interrupted, but I grabbed his arm and pulled him back.

"You murdered my husband. In cold blood.''

"I am going to ask you to leave, Marylin. Please, everybody out. This has gone far enough.''

"Anna knows,'' Marylin shouted. "She'll show you. Show him! Prove it!''

Stepping to the center of the room, I opened my briefcase, took out the flasher, and laid it on the trestle table. "This is what killed Henry Brook,'' I said. "There was no lightning, Gloria. This is what you saw. Rigged up to the lights at the end of the jetty, it created a lightning-like flicker. What was just a pretty effect for most people was enough to trigger a seizure for someone suffering from photic or light-sensitive epilepsy.''

There was an instant sensation. Rossol said, "You've made a bad mistake. One you're going to regret.''

"Mrs. Brook,'' I asked, "did your husband suffer from epilepsy?''

"He did. And very few knew about it. This damn picture—lights, special effects, battle scenes.'' She whirled to Rossol. "You knew. You knew, and you involved Belinda."

"Belinda involved herself," he said cruelly, and for the first time I was apprehensive about the outcome.

"It wasn't my fault," the girl cried, terrified. "It wasn't my fault."

"The flasher did not operate all the time," I continued. "There must have been a switch. When Brook was maneuvered out onto the jetty, it was turned on, provoking a seizure. He collapsed and was pushed into the water. Then the flasher was turned off. The heat lightning disappeared—and so did Henry Brook."

"It can't be," Gloria pleaded. "It was lightning. And Len wasn't gone long. Not long at all. It wasn't you, Len, it wasn't." She extended a tentative, imploring hand, which he ignored.

"No," he replied, "no, technically, it wasn't. Was it, Belinda? Little Miss Do It Her Own Way. You wanted to see the trick, didn't you? You stayed around to help him look. When he collapsed, you panicked. And being neurotic and psychotic and all the rest, you threw one of your fits. When I reached him, he was already in the water, and you were crying some nonsense about killing your father." As he spoke, he looked not at Belinda, standing numbed and terrified, but at Marylin, who closed her eyes in anguish.

"And what made him collapse?" I asked as everything started to fall apart. "Who rigged that circuit? And who almost killed the caretaker trying to get the flasher back?"

Gloria put her hand over her mouth. "Oh, please, Len!" She stepped toward him, but unlike Dr. Kleinz, Len Rossol was not to have fine speeches, excuses, justifications: even Belinda was not quite enough.

"Leave me alone!" When Gloria tried to stop him, he struck her, sending her tumbling backwards. Harry yelled and grabbed for him, but Rossol was out the door and down the steps before the rest could react. Gloria slumped on the floor with her face in her hands, and for an instant all we heard was Belinda's convulsive weeping. Marylin screamed as if her throat was tearing. "But it's his fault. She'd never have done any harm. He knew her problems. He knew!" Her pain turned to revenge and she shouted, "Stop him! Stop him!"

I blocked the door. "A minute. Wait a minute."

They were starting to argue when the scream came. I jumped off the step and sprinted toward the hill. There was another cry, a low, throaty growling and a frantic appeal for help. "Hector! Down! Help me! I can't hold him!"

"Oh, my God!" said Valon, stopping in surprise. "It'll kill him."

The mastiff was dragging the caretaker across the lawn in its struggle to get at Rossol, who had stumbled—or jumped—over the low garden wall. There was blood on the director's trousers and hands, and he was frantically trying to get back on his feet and elude the frenzied dog.

"I can't hold him," Arthur cried, as the dog lunged again and again, each time jerking the slight caretaker forward and almost off his feet. Harry raced past me and seized the leash, his weight drawing the powerful dog up short.

"Be careful," I shouted, afraid he would be attacked in turn, but the mastiff ignored him. The animal's whole interest was fixed on Rossol, and it strained forward, barking and snarling in fury and frustration as two of the crew ran around the wall and lifted the director to his feet.

"That brute should be muzzled," Valon exclaimed indignantly. "Look at Rossol's hand."

"He's never done anything like this," Arthur protested between gasps of breath. "He would never have been allowed loose had there been the slightest—" He broke off and shook his head. "Right enough, he saw Mr. Rossol running, but—"

"Rossol's special," I said. "Whatever happened that night on the jetty, he was the one who set the flasher and the one who tried to recover it. Hector attacked him without warning because he recognized the man who almost killed his master."

SIXTEEN

A TINY STRIP of the Connecticut River was visible from Valon's window, and I could just make out a thin white line of rotting ice along the shore. Spring was coming late. Had *The Lazarus Gambit* been scheduled for this year, it would have been far too cold for a summerhouse party, and Henry Brook might have lived to write his memoirs. Behind me, Valon's lighter clicked; the odor of his cigarette filled the office, and his leather chair creaked with a lazy, satisfied sound. Except for our height above the city, we might have been in some cozy men's club ready for a drowsy afternoon. We had already been extravagantly feted in the executive dining rooms. There had been toasts and speeches, and I had been the recipient of a fat check: *The Lazarus Gambit* investigation was closed at last. The case had run so long and my fee had grown so large that I had flown north to collect it ceremonially at the home office.

"A long time," Valon remarked like an echo.

"Just what I was thinking."

It had been a circus, in fact. The revelations about the death of Henry Brook had dominated the gossip, fan, and sensation publications for months. The trial had provided another gold mine, starting with technical details of circuits, flashers, and switches, which finally convinced the public and jury that the murder had been premeditated, and proceeding through the exertions of psychiatrists and therapists who had attempted to determine such imponderables as whether Leonard Rossol possessed moral sense or Belinda Tayana a split personality. One squad of experts claimed the latter was a psychopathic personality in the grip of an Electra complex, a diagnosis that produced some confusion and many dreadful puns. This contingent was staunchly opposed by a second illustrious crew who claimed that Belinda's forgetfulness on the witness stand was the result of profound emotional trauma, making it impossible for her to defend herself against "the scurrilous charges of an unscrupulous defense," as her lawyers put it. The whole trial was conducted according to the very highest standards of the dramatic, if not the judicial art, and few were spared sensational and unsavory revelations. I had quite expected to find a little bilge coming my way, but perhaps foolishly, Rossol's lawyer had preferred to concentrate on Belinda, "the real murderer in this tragedy."

This view had certain things in its favor, including Belinda's emotional problems, her difficulties with her parents, and her "unusual relationship" with the late Henry Brook. But ultimately, material evidence outweighed high-flown theories, and the flasher proved too much for the jury to swallow. Along with Marylin Brook's staunch support of her protégée, the electrical device proved more potent than references to patricide and the ill-fated Electra.

Of course, Mrs. Brook's partisanship could be interpreted in more than one way, but the distinguished counsel for the defense was generally considered to have made a mistake when he accused her of plotting her husband's demise with Belinda, her protégée and his lover. This was going too far, and Marylin Brook was never better than when she was on the offensive. Her belligerence and stamina made her a formidable courtroom opponent, and even the public, initially suspicious, began to transform her from an intolerable battle-ax to an admirable battler. I suspect neither Marylin's excellent public relations sense nor her press contacts hindered this favorable evolution.

Throughout, like other famous trials, the "Lazarus" murder case proved a litmus test for opinion. Belinda and Marylin were made to order for feminist theorists, provided their theories didn't probe too far beneath the surface. Len Rossol presented a less pat case, though certain conservatives painted him as a man done in by chivalry—of all things. Those who were pious saw the case as evidence of the breakdown of values; those who were not saw it as a consequence of "fast-track" lives and other linguistic abominations. The superstitious were especially blessed: "Curses! Jinx! Spiritual influences!" screamed the papers in the supermarket racks. It was a very dull cast or crew member who didn't pocket at least a modest sum for a reminiscence, interview, or article, with coverage ranging from atmospheric shots of the *Gambit* sites to one extra's "I knew There Was a Devil on the Set" story, which enjoyed a full week's celebrity. Lani Dupres became an overnight talk-show fixture with her "I was the last to perform with Henry Brook" bit polished to perfection. Her success provoked Altheia Karl to enter the lists with a sensible and debunking interview, which met with a much less favorable response. Common sense was not in high demand around the "Lazarus" murder case.

In the end, a great many people made money. Probably enough, all told, to have saved Rossol's studio, spared Henry Brook, and completed the film. The boom lasted for months, and at its height one of the major networks purchased full rights to the documentary at a fabulous price. Fortunately, Rossol had been able to edit the footage while he was out on bail, and it wound up on prime time with a voice-over by one of our most mellifluous and distinguished newscasters. Once again Rossol was hailed as a genius, and much ink was expended on art and death in the modern world and on what one pretentious popular magazine called "the arrogance of talent." Quickie books were rushed into print to inform us still further, the original novel returned "triumphantly" to the bestseller lists, and even I was approached for an "inside story."

If there was anything that these pundits and commentators agreed on, it was that no one could hold center stage better than Len Rossol. Yet that old pro forgot the adage about the theatrical dangers of children and dogs. I knew he was in trouble when I saw Belinda the first morning of the trial. Gone was the sophisticate with the midnight eyes and garnet lipstick. Instead, there was what appeared to be a pretty, rather delicate child of thirteen or fourteen, gotten up in the simplest of pastel dresses. These outfits, her perfect diction, and flawless manners went a long way to excusing such foibles as a precocious sex life (conveniently blamed on Mother) and memory lapses (the fault of Father). Her quite genuine anguish and anxiety won the jury. If there were any lingering doubts about what so troubled a young woman might or might not have done, they were quite erased by the last witness, who was led in by a burly K-9 specialist. Hector's calm and decorum were evident to all, and, in a clever ploy, the defense lawyer was asked to hold his leash to ensure there was no trickery. All this tranquility evaporated as soon as the animal was led close enough to recognize Rossol. Instantly, he broke into savage growls and snarls, greatly impressing the spectators and leading the prosecution to some very flowery language about the loyalty of dumb animals, while Arthur McNab sat and nodded in the balcony. There was never any doubt after this that Rossol would be found guilty of aggravated assault and only very skillful defense work kept him from picking up an additional attempted murder charge.

Hector also swayed the guilty verdict on the much more serious Brook conspiracy-and-murder charge, although knowledgeable court watchers and journalists conceded that the investigation conducted by Independence Mutual had really built the case. With these endorsements, my past errors and transgressions were forgiven. ''We're saving you money!'' began a new Independence Mutual ad series, and my perspicacity and perseverance were lauded to the skies by none other than company president R. Cecil Woodward. When all the fancy bookkeeping was finished, my net worth was considerably enhanced, and I had garnered a fortune in free publicity. To any sensible person this was a satisfactory ending to a troublesome case.

Valon cleared his throat, ''Woodward—and everyone—was really very pleased," he said, delicately picking a speck of tobacco from his lower lip.

"And well they should be. They got off easy."

"We seem to have done all right out of a nasty mess," Valon admitted.

"I suppose we fit in with the opportunists. The less scrupulous, of course, really cleaned up."

"You're a bit cynical."

"Don't give me the 'social benefits of insurance' speech; I've heard it already today. You're like me—a few more scruples and better manners but not quite hypocritical enough to swallow the party line."

Valon looked down his long, straight nose and considered taking offense, then dusted the ash off his cigarette and nodded. "I wonder what's to happen to that Belinda Tayana."

"I should ask you. She's been here in town at the Institute, hasn't she?" It had been considered prudent to pack her off to a respectable private mental hospital for rest and therapy.

"So I understand. I meant with all the fuss."

The fuss was a flood of offers—to write books, to authorize a television show, to consent to a movie. *The Belinda Tayana Story* in caps and lights: sex, scandal, heartbreak, glamour—and possibly murder? "Her mama's after a chunk of the money," I said.

"Really?"

"Appeared out of the West with tears and lawyers. I'd like to be ringside when she and Marylin Brook go after the movie rights."

"The girl's of age now."

"She needs someone to take care of her—in consequence, I suppose, of her bizarre early life. I'm rather rooting for Marylin. She's a Gorgon, but no one will take advantage of Belinda with her around.''

"If we'd just turned the flasher over to the police," Valon said cautiously, "Miss Tayana might never have been mentioned.''

"That's true. We might not have closed the case against Rossol, either.''

He sat forward and folded his hands on the desk. "Was that the only reason for your little theatrical?''

I looked out at the ice on the river. It was none of his business, but I said, "No, I owed Rossol. I saw a chance to get him, and I took it. The business about Belinda came as a complete surprise.''

"Woodward feels you take an overly personal approach," Valon said reflectively, and I began to suspect he'd had more than his usual luncheon martini.

"Investigation isn't an exact science. If you get out from behind your desk and get to know people, you become involved with them, sometimes unpleasantly for all concerned." I thought of Gloria and Belinda, the casualties of my success.

"'Personal detection' Cecil calls it. Very feminine.''

I wanted to say that R. Cecil Woodward was a well-known ass but controlled myself. "Is there any other kind of detection?''

"I don't think we'll hire you again," Valon remarked now. "Personally, I'm sorry, but I think it's unlikely. The company's never approved of mess.''

So that was why he'd seemed thoughtful; he'd been delegated to give me the bad news. "I thought that's why they hired me—to avoid mess.''

"They wanted none at all, it seems. If it were up

to me—'' he shrugged—''but I've been promoted out
of the whole area.''

"Congratulations are in order." I reached over the
desk to shake his hand.

"Thank you, Anna. Awkward under the circumstances, as you can imagine."

"At the moment, thanks to all this, I've more business than I can handle."

"I'm glad to hear that." His cigarette, neglected,
burned to ash in the tray.

"It's time I got going for my plane," I said, gathering my belongings.

Valon looked up quickly. "Did she do it?"

"What?"

"Did Miss Tayana kill Brook?"

"The jury decided that, Alex."

"The guests at the show, you mean."

"She and Rossol were pretty evenly matched: experts, character witnesses, everything but astrologers
and graphologists."

"You know," Valon said.

"No, I don't know. I have ideas but I don't know.
I know Rossol planned to murder Brook; I know he
set the flasher and maneuvered him out onto the jetty.
What really happened that night—your guess is as
good as mine. And that's all it is, a guess. They were
both capable."

"Yes?"

"And that's not opinion." Nonetheless, I was glad
my cross-examination had never gotten around to the
day Belinda very nearly skewered me with a chef's
knife. To be evenhanded, I had said nothing, either,

about Rossol's little farce with the pistol. That was the best I could do.

"It seems agreed that his sentence would have been longer if there hadn't been that doubt," Valon said unhappily.

"Remember, if there had been too much doubt, Independence Mutual would have wound up paying the bills."

"I just wondered if we didn't perhaps...distort what we saw." He looked at me, wanting an answer. Too bad he'd just fired me.

"That's always the danger. Tell Woodward there's always some mess. He'll have to accept that." I started toward the door.

"But did she do it?" Valon asked again.

"Do you want me to reopen the case?"

"I have no authority to do that."

"Then you'll just have to settle for the verdict. Rossol willed Brook's death, whether he actually carried it out or not."

Valon rose and came forward in some agitation. "Yes, he wanted it, but is that enough?"

I reached out and shook his hand. "Alex," I said, "now you've left detection and entered philosophy."

He opened the door automatically. On the way downstairs, I thought that Rossol had gotten a story befitting a genius and an artist. If less dramatic than Dr. Kleinz's pulp thriller, it was full of surprising twists, touched with irony, and ended in ambiguity. Belinda was a different matter. For her, we'd have to wait, and I thought it would be interesting to see how *The Belinda Tayana Story* turned out.

HARLEQUIN®

I N T R I G U E®

When little Adam Kingsley was taken from his nursery in the Kingsley mansion, the Memphis family used all their power and prestige to punish the kidnapper. They believed the crime was solved and the villain condemned...though the boy was never returned. But now, new evidence comes to light that may reveal the truth about...

The Kingsley Baby

Amanda Stevens is at her best for this powerful trilogy of a sensational crime and the three couples whose love lights the way to the truth. Don't miss:

#453 THE HERO'S SON (February)
#458 THE BROTHER'S WIFE (March)
#462 THE LONG-LOST HEIR (April)

What *really* happened that night in the Kingsley nursery?

HINKING